ILLUSTRATIONS BY
LAILA EKBOIR

PAMELA EHRENBERG
& TRACY LÓPEZ

DETOUR
AHEAD

BRUNO'S BICY
& R

PANADER
ARACEL

Written by Pamela Ehrenberg and Tracy López

Text copyright © 2022 Harold Grinspoon Foundation

Illustration and cover art copyright © 2022 Laila Ekboir

Published in 2022 by PJ Publishing, an imprint of PJ Library

ISBN:978-1-7365573-5-8

Library of Congress Control Number: 2021949369

Edited by Karen Ang

Book design by Chad W. Beckerman

PJ Publishing creates board books, picture books, chapter books, and graphic novels in multiple languages that represent the diversity of Jewish families today. By sharing Jewish narratives, values, and life events, we help families explore their connections with Jewish life.

For information regarding permissions, please email permissions@hgf.org or contact us at:

PJ Library, a program of the Harold Grinspoon Foundation

67 Hunt Street, Suite 100

Agawam, MA 01001 USA

Printed in China

FOR DAVID GREBOW, MY
FIRST AND BEST
WRITING TEACHER
— P.M.E.

FOR NICOLAS
AND JULIAN
— T.L.

GILAH

BUS STOP

This is the corner of Porter Street and Connecticut Avenue Northwest: a regular, ordinary street corner in Washington, DC, where I wait every morning for the regular, ordinary Metrobus that takes me to my school. The part that is not ordinary is that my mom is not waiting here with me like she did at the beginning of the school year, because as of today I am allowed to take the bus by myself.

I'm at the corner early, with my eyes glued in the direction the bus will be coming from, so I can't possibly miss it even if my mind is thinking of other things. Here are some of the things I am thinking about:

- breakdancing moves
- music that is good for breakdancing
- the Hebrew I am studying for my bat mitzvah coming up—and which of the letters look most like breakdancing moves.

I am not thinking about my mom smiling and taking pictures from the window of our house, which she will probably text to my dad at work as soon as I get on the bus. Even though my mom always tells me not to take pictures at the wrong time, she keeps taking pictures of me that I don't like—I think she forgets that I'm not five. If the bus thing goes well, she is starting a new job next week, the first one since my sister Miri was born. I don't know whether we'll cheer and take pictures of her leaving for work.

I've been waiting for six minutes when my sister Miri comes outside and crosses the street for her bus, which is also a regular, ordinary Metrobus but filled mostly with kids from her middle school. The rainbow peace sign key chain on her backpack is what's called a visual cue that she is still eleven. As in, one and a half years younger than me. As in, people my age think they are too old for a key chain like that. It is not a visual cue having to do with actual peacefulness, as anyone would know if they heard Miri this morning when the tie-dye shirt that she needed right that second for school spirit day happened to be in the wash.

Her bus goes the opposite direction from mine. Sometimes I wonder if we are going opposite ways from each other even when we're not on the bus.

My brother Asher goes to a regular high school, except it is not very regular that he gets there at seven thirty in the morning for chess club.

Miri's bus comes first, like we practiced.

My bus comes second, like we practiced.

I am facing the right direction so I'm sure to notice when it comes, just like we practiced.

Except for one thing that is not like we practiced.

The bus to my school says "H4" on the front. *Not in service* means the bus is broken—not breaking like dancing, but broken like maybe the engine might overheat or a wheel is about to fall off. It's probably going someplace to get fixed, which is not my school because I'm pretty sure no one there knows how to fix buses.

This bus is filled with regular people, just like the H4. But it doesn't say "H4," it says "Not In Service."

People are crowding around me, pushing to get on the NOT IN SERVICE bus. In case they didn't see the sign in capital-letter lights, I yell (also in capital letters), "THIS BUS IS NOT IN SERVICE."

A few people smile as they keep pushing on.

My brother Asher tried to teach me about smiling by making two flash cards that didn't really work.

But when people are moving and smiling at the same time, it's hard to get a good look before you have to look away or else you will be staring. I didn't tell Asher that his flash cards weren't actually that helpful because I didn't want him to feel bad after he'd gone to all that trouble.

In any case, whether these people on the bus are smiling to be my friend or smiling to be jerks who are not worth my time, I really don't want a new friend right now, I want the H4 bus to take me to my school.

"You're blocking the door," says the driver, which is a fact but not an instruction because he hasn't said where he wants me to be instead.

"You're blocking the door!" he says louder, like I didn't hear him the first time.

"IT'S NOT IN SERVICE!" I shout back, in case it's Say Obvious Things Loudly for No Reason Day.

"The sign's broken," the driver says. "You see the bus is in service, so get on or stop blocking the door."

Actually, I didn't see the bus is in service, because I didn't look under the hood, and even if I did, I wouldn't know what to look for. But if *he* has inside information that the bus is in service, that would have been helpful to share at the beginning. Way more helpful than shouting about me blocking the door without saying what he wants me to do instead.

I climb on and tap my DC One card on the fare box.

"Sheesh," I hear someone say as I walk back to find a seat.

Maybe they were sheesh-ing me, but I think we all should be sheesh-ing the driver: why did he have to make things complicated by waiting to mention the sign was wrong?

WINDOW

Filling up seats on a bus is like a video game where each person sits one at a time in the two-seaters until there's a person in every two-seater and then the aisle seats start getting filled. When my mom and I did our practice rides, I asked why she didn't sit in front of me or behind me, so she explained that the rules change if you get on with someone you know.

One rule that does not change is that the poles are only for helping people stay balanced in case there is not a seat available while the bus is moving (or possibly the only seat available is in the back, so people may need to walk down the aisle while the bus is moving). It is not OK to use the poles for a breakdancing routine like I've seen people do on YouTube because it is not safe to breakdance on a moving bus.

The plexiglass window feels cool and kind of relaxes that

side of my head. Sometimes, when I have to do something hard at school—the kind of thing that can make my brain hurt enough to have a meltdown—I press my head against something cool and imagine I'm on the bus with the cool window.

Some examples of things that are on the other side of the window are:

- houses
- parked cars
- the bank that gives me ten dollars each year in their summer reading program
- a man playing guitar next to a bucket where people throw money

Basically, regular stuff.

Until something happens outside the window that is the opposite of regular.

The bus passes just a few inches from a boy in a many-colored jacket who is riding a bike. He falls off and lands between two parked cars.

He does not get up right away, which could mean he is hurt really badly, even though he is wearing a helmet, because helmets are not magic, and people do not usually stop riding their bike in

the middle of traffic and decide to lie down for a nap, because that would not be safe, even with a helmet. And also, he is wearing a backpack (which is now sort of on top of his many-colored coat), which probably means he is going to school.

If he is lying down on the road between two parked cars instead of riding his bicycle like he was a second ago, there is a good chance he is hurt.

"Someone fell off a bike!" I yell. When no one answers, I yell again, in capital letters, "SOMEONE FELL OFF A BIKE!"

STOP

"SOMEONE FELL OFF A BIKE!"

I don't know how many times I yell. Sometimes it is OK to yell, such as at a football game and when someone is bleeding.

We are not at a football game, but I don't know if someone is bleeding. When I've fallen off my bike, sometimes I am bleeding and sometimes not.

The boy's jacket has all kinds of colors on it. He is like Joseph in the many-colored coat, which is a story in the Torah that I am studying for my bat mitzvah. Joseph's coat had blood on it, adding to its many colors. I can't tell if this boy's coat has blood added to it or not.

The bus stops.

The bus is not supposed to stop in the middle of the street.

But the bus is not supposed to keep going when someone is hurt.

I hate when the two things that are not supposed to happen are the opposite of each other. That makes my whole body feel like it's stopped too, just like the bus, even though I know my heart is still beating.

I am going to be late to school.

I look around to see who is in charge.

The bus driver is in charge of driving the bus.

The passengers are in charge of riding to school or work.

No one is in charge of helping a boy who fell off a bike.

I see that the people around me are looking around too. It's a nice feeling to see everyone doing what I am already doing, rather than me trying to be more like them.

"I'll see if he's OK," says a man across the aisle. I wonder if he is a doctor—in which case, he should have gotten off the bus sooner. Maybe he is new at being a doctor and forgot at first that he is the one who's supposed to help.

As the maybe doctor gets off the bus, the boy sits up and looks around. He is not covered with blood. The maybe doctor does not take any doctor things out of his bag.

The boy stands up, leans on his bike, and removes his helmet. If he is standing, he is not badly hurt, but if he is leaning, he might be a little bit hurt. I notice his hair is dark and neat like from a comb, not messed up at all from falling off his bike, except for a piece that sticks up a little in the back, but that might be a cowlick, which is a piece that always sticks up. I don't know, because I'm only seeing him right now and didn't see him before he fell off his bike.

SMILE

After the man gets off the bus, the driver grumbles about what will probably happen. "He'll probably make something up. Probably call Metro. Now I gotta call this in. This could take a while."

Sometimes when someone gets hurt at school, someone else says that they are making it up for attention, but usually that is not true. I hope this boy is OK.

It would be nice to know, like this bus driver seemed to, when someone might probably make something up.

It would also be nice if the driver said who he would probably call, such as the people at the Metrobus office. I like when things are specific.

One after another, people get off to catch another bus. Some people are shaking their heads. But I stay in my seat. I get off at the corner with the Five Below store and the T&D Bank. No place else. That's how I get to school.

Not many people are left on the bus now, just me and the driver and a guy wearing headphones. Someone else is outside the bus, though: the boy who fell off his bike.

He's on the sidewalk, looking through the bus windows with his hands cupped around his eyes. I don't know why.

He's walking along the side of the bus, but he stops when he gets to the window next to my seat. He looks at me and smiles, for some reason.

But the rule is that if another kid smiles at you—if they are not smiling to be a jerk who is not worth your time, and if they are not a grown-up you don't know, who has no reason to smile at an almost-teenager and their smile does not make you uncomfortable—then it is nice to smile back. So I do.

That's when he mouths, "Thank you."

When someone says, "Thank you," the answer is sometimes, "You're welcome." Although sometimes the right answer is "No problem," if you are under twenty or "My pleasure," if you are twenty-one or older. (The year I am exactly twenty, I will just hope no one thanks me for anything.) I mouth, "You're welcome," back to him before I start to wonder if I should have picked one of the other answers instead.

GUILLERMO

GUILLERMO ALAS

Guillermo, don't be a sabelotodo—a know-it-all, she says, but
Underneath my mother's don't-mess-with-me face
Is a smile
Like a wildflower pushing through a crack in the sidewalk.
Like mother, like son, my father would say,
Except he's not here right now. Every day he
Rises before the sun, goes to his panadería,
Makes a dozen different types of breads, cookies, and cakes
Overnight, while my mother, little sister, and I sleep.
And some days,
Like today, I ride my bike there before school,
A backpack on my back, a poem in my head,
Speeding toward the sweet scent of bread in the chilly morning
  air.

PANADERÍA ARACELI

Bronze bells chime against the glass-paned door.
Warm sugared air promises sweet things.
Pastel turquoise and tangerine walls,
and the soft glow of lights in empty cases.
I love coming to Panadería Araceli
(named after my little sister)
before sunrise.

In the kitchen I find my father,
sleeves rolled to his elbows,
and copy his thick hands kneading the dough
while he tells me stories I've heard
a million times before
about how he learned everything from his Tía Claudia
at her bakery in El Salvador,
and how there was a chucho aguacatero they named Canela
who would sleep just inside the doorway
curled like the churros españoles they sell
during Fiestas Agostinas.

From my father I have learned to make:
semita de guayaba with a crisscross pattern across the top,
orejitas, crispy and sticky,
quesadillas sprinkled with sesame seeds, and
pastelitos de piña, filled with pineapple jam.

Someday I'll tell my kids stories too,
and I'll try not to tell them a million times.
I think he does it
not just so I don't forget where he came from,
but so he doesn't either.

THE FIRE

PART I

This is not our first bakery.
Our first bakery
burned down one night.
Burned down until
all that was left
was a black skeleton
of charred wood
still smoking
and my reflection
in the steel mixing bowl
in the middle of it all.

PART II

In the woods
behind the strip mall
a campfire
became a wildfire
and we lost everything.

Well, not everything.

Everything at the bakery.
My family was safe.
That's what my mother
kept reminding us,
every time Araceli
had nightmares.

When my parents
received the insurance money
instead of rebuilding
in the same place
where there are a half dozen

other panaderías

within just a couple miles,

they decided

it was a good opportunity

to start a bakery

in a neighborhood that

didn't have one,

a good opportunity

to start over

somewhere else.

That somewhere else

turned out to be here

in Washington, DC.

The only problem is,

nobody asked me.

THE COAT

The coat I'm wearing
is not the coat
I want
to be wearing,
but when my father asked,
"¿Y tu chumpa?"
and I told him
I can't find it
because it's still packed in boxes
from our move,
he told me,
"take mine,"
and pointed with his lips
to his blue wool sweater-like jacket
with zigzags
and stripes
in colors
I've seen
on tropical birds
at the National Zoo:

scarlet macaw red

flamingo pink

peacock green.

"I'm not cold," I say

knowing before the words

leave my mouth

what he'll say in response.

"Ponétela."

Three words in one.

Put it on.

And I know

there's no use in arguing

so I

put it on

and ride my bike

face down

watching the blur of the sidewalk

beneath my pedals.

CRASH

PART I

I didn't see the bus
and the bus didn't see me
or rather the driver
since buses don't have eyes to see.

I didn't see the bus
until the bumper
bumped my tire,
and twisted my handlebars
out of my grasp.

I didn't see the bus,
but saw instead
my palms, red,
and felt the sting
of slapping the cement.

PART II

Palms red,
like my cheeks,
everyone stops
to look at me.

Horns blare
beep-beep-beeeeeep!
I hurry to stand
on shaky feet
because what if Dad hears
all this commotion
what if he sees
my bike on the street
broken?

He'll say things like,
"Didn't I teach you to look both ways?
That streetlights and signs must be obeyed?
To be on your toes,
and to always pay attention?

Are you listening, hijo?

Avoiding a tragedy

starts with prevention.

Where was your head?

What were you thinking?

Ey, answer when I ask you a question.

Don't just stand there silent and blinking.

You're lucky you're not lying here

outlined in chalk.

Ey, you know better than that,

Guillermo,

quiet when I talk."

Then when Mom finds out,

(and of course she will)

she'll say things like,

"Memo!

You could have been killed!"

And then they'll both say,

"We know how much you like to explore,

but we think it would be better

if you didn't ride your bicycle around
by yourself anymore."

And that
at the end of the day
is the absolute worst thing
my parents could say.

PART III

Last summer
like every summer before
I rode my bicycle
with my primos,
Mayra, Alex, Lucas,
Bernardo, and Nelson,
but not Sofía,
because she's little,
like my sister.

Last summer
like every summer before
we rode our bicycles
miles and miles
around Langley Park,
and to my family's bakery
to wipe down the front windows,
sweep the sidewalk,
and break down cardboard boxes,
in exchange for a little pocket money.

Last summer
like every summer before
we rode our bicycles
to La Union Mall
to walk around,
and eat paletas
in flavors like
arroz con leche,
watermelon, mango,
and chamoy,
which is a Mexican chile sauce

that is sweet, salty, sour, and spicy
all at once.

Last summer
like every summer before
we rode our bicycles
to the park
to play fútbol
and basketball,
or we'd take stale tortillas
to feed the ducks,
until Mayra learned
that bread and tortillas
(stale or otherwise)
aren't good for them,
so we'd bring corn or peas instead,
then run screaming and laughing
when they flapped their feathered wings
or got too close.

Last summer
like every summer before

we rode our bicycles
to each other's houses,
for late-night barbecues,
our tías and tíos
laughing and dancing
to cumbia,
stars twinkling in blue darkness
that smelled like carne asada.

But last summer
was my last summer
there.

It's weird,
but I feel like
somehow
my bicycle remembers too.

PART IV

"Are you OK?"
The bus is stopped,

and a guy with copper-colored hair,
freckles,
and a plaid scarf around his neck
strides right up to me.
I stare at his spotless shoes.

"You OK, bro?"
I nod, and stand up.
He sets his messenger bag down,
lifts my bike, and
straightens the handlebars.

"The way that girl was freaking out,
I thought you'd be flat as a pancake,"
he laughs, then shakes his head.
"Which girl?" I ask,
and he jabs a thumb toward the bus.

I look up
into tinted windows
with hands cupped
around my eyes so I can see.

Her face is a pale oval
and her hair like a frizzy halo.
"Thank you," I say,
even though she can't hear me.

She blinks
and then
I think
she says,
"You're welcome."

GILAH

ARRIVAL

It takes a long time until the bus starts moving again. I don't know what time it is, since my phone is off and it's not like the sun's position in the sky will be all that different if I'm late for school.

Eight forty-five is when our class starts our morning meeting.

I don't think I'll be late enough to miss geometry, which comes after that. That happens sometimes, when kids come late—but not me. If I'm late, I not only miss the one class where math and art turn out to be the same thing but I also spend the whole day being a step behind everyone else.

When the bus finally reaches my stop, it is another time when two opposites are supposed to happen at the same time:

(a) I am supposed to be on time for school.

(b) I am supposed to wait for a "walk" signal, check for traffic in both directions, and proceed with caution across the street.

(It doesn't help that people seem to be always on the lookout for my breaking a rule, even when the rules contradict each other and there is literally no way to avoid breaking at least one rule.)

Sometimes opposites get jumbled together in my brain. When that happens, I might race across Fourteenth Street without paying as much attention as usual to cars turning right from Irving Street. I might hear someone screech on their brakes and someone else yell in Spanish, which is a language I hear a lot in the neighborhood where my school is.

When I get inside, my school is calm.

"AM I LATE?" I yell to Ms. Quattlebaum before she even says, "Good morning, Gilah," which is how she starts every single day.

"Good morning, Gilah," says Ms. Quattlebaum, smiling her same smile. "No, you're not late, though I was just starting to wonder since you're always on time. You need to be careful crossing Fourteenth Street, though. It's better to be late if being on time would be dangerous!"

"Yeah," I agree. "The bus had to stop so the driver could make a phone call."

"My train was running late this morning too," says Ms. Quattlebaum. "That always makes me feel like my whole day is mixed up."

"Yeah!" I agree again.

"OK, well, head on up to class then, before Mr. Muser starts wondering too. I'll see you when you come down for art."

"SEE YOU!" I yell, heading upstairs for geometry.

COLLAGE

If geometry is kind of like math as art, then the only thing better is actual art class.

Today I move my clothespin to the collage center, where there is glitter paper, tissue paper, foam stick-on paper, and other kinds of paper that don't have names. (The reason we have clothespins in art class is to keep track of who's using which materials, so it's easy to figure out if someone is actually done with whatever materials are lying on the table next to them. People were having meltdowns because other people were taking materials that they thought people were done with, so some other kids and I made up a system with clothespins so it would be obvious who was using what. And now we get to spend more time actually making art.) Without exactly planning it, I end up with a silver square on top of a bigger blue square. It's not a coincidence, as everyone in my family has been seeing squares like this all over the house for weeks. These are the exact colors of my bat mitzvah invitation.

I spend the whole art time adding details, making the invitation much more interesting than the real ones, with little doodles of breakdancing moves in the corners and about ten kinds of lettering that I copy from an *I Can Do Calligraphy* book. It helps that I  can remember the actual invitation, calling it up in my mind like a picture on my phone, so I put all the stuff on there like the name of the synagogue and what time and the party at the hotel.

I started working on the invitation just as a piece of art, but after I'm done it feels silly to waste it. Like maybe there's somebody who the rest of my family doesn't know but who I might want to invite. And who might actually like a homemade invitation better than an "official" one anyway.

STRENGTH-TRAINING

One boy who is of course on the list for my bat mitzvah is the kid of my mom's friend. They call Noam my friend even though he isn't, really. He and I started kindergarten together at the Brandywine School, and my mom was friends with his mom, which meant we had a lot of playdates.

By *playdates,* I mean that I played on the swing set in Noam's backyard while Noam organized his Pokémon cards in the plastic play house. What made it a playdate was that we came over on a particular date so our moms could drink coffee.

For someone who still gets driven around everywhere instead of taking the bus on his own, Noam likes to act like he has life all figured out. Especially my life. For instance, on Monday morning in P.E. he tells me:

- "You shouldn't do too many pull-ups on those rings. What if your muscles get so big that your bat mitzvah dress doesn't fit?"
- "Are those even the same muscles you use to do a backflip in breakdancing? I bet you didn't even look to see if those are the right muscles you need."

- "I've never heard of breakdancing as a bat mitzvah thing. When I had my bar mitzvah in Israel, I did not see one single person breakdancing at the Western Wall."

"CAN YOU PLEASE FIND SOMETHING APPRO-PRIATE TO FOCUS ON?" I tell him. Because it is really not worth my time to explain how his comments are sexist and obviously uninformed about my breakdancing and about the many ways there are to have a bat mitzvah.

SEATS

When the bus after school stops at the Hughes Academic Campus, lots of kids my age and my brother's and sister's ages pile in. Then we have to wait while the driver gets out to attach someone's bike to the front of the bus, even though people who take their bikes on a Metrobus are supposed to do this themselves.

(My brother Asher tells me not to get so mad when other people break rules, that sometimes they have reasons other people don't know about. But people don't seem to think that's true for me. I think anyone who spends as much time as I do trying to figure out what the rules even are has a right to get annoyed when other people's disregard for the rules makes me late getting home.)

I'm paying attention to the bike, watching how the driver has to fit it in on the rack, so I don't stop to think about whether the bike is connected to a person. But then, at the exact same time, I see the twisted bike and then the boy who belongs to it.

He is wearing the jacket of many colors.

I don't know the odds, maybe one in a million, or maybe better than that if his school ends the same time as mine and he doesn't usually ride the bus because he usually rides his bike. But even if the odds are only one in a hundred, only one in fifty—it still feels like good luck.

I look around the bus. Besides the empty seat next to me, there are probably seven or eight more empty seats around the bus. But not two together, which is the rule. As long as there aren't two empty seats together, the boy in the coat of many colors might sit next to someone. Might sit next to me.

My jacket is just blue fleece—recognizable by the larger-than-usual number of pockets and smaller-than-usual number of tags—not something memorable like the coat of many colors. What if he doesn't recognize me? What's the rule about what to say to someone when you sort of saved their life earlier but didn't learn their name?

My heart's beating faster, and I'm breathing faster too, as he climbs up the steps, the last kid from his school, and taps his DC One card. *Beep.*

HELLO

The rule is, if someone sits next to you on the bus, you don't say, "Hello my name is ___." Because if you have to say your name, that means you don't already know them, and people do not like to talk to people they don't already know while they are riding a bus. If you see someone you happen to know, then it is OK to say hello, but then you would not say your name.

The jacket of many colors is very close to my jacket of one color, but I'm still thinking about whether the boy wearing the jacket is someone I know when the boy says, "Hi."

If another kid says hi—if they are not smiling to be a jerk who is not worth your time and who has no reason to say hi to an almost-teenager and their "hi" does not make you uncomfortable—then it is nice to say "hi" back.

"Hi," I say back.

He says, "Thanks for your help this morning. I heard that out of all those people, you were the one who stopped the bus for me."

I remember that this morning I answered, "You're welcome," but wasn't sure that was the right thing to say.

He doesn't seem mad about the way I answered.

"Are you OK?" I ask, since that is what I want to know now.

"Me, yes. My bike, not so much," he says.

"That's terrible," I say. Then I add, "About the bike," in case he thinks I think it's terrible that he's OK.

He smiles, and it is not a jerk-who-is-not-worth-my-time smile, but I can't tell if it's exactly a friend smile. Maybe there's another kind of smile for when something bad happens (a broken bike) but something worse doesn't happen (getting hurt), and something maybe a little bit good happens (someone on the bus being sympathetic about the bike), all at the same time.

"My name's Guillermo," he says.

That would usually be an easy one, except I'm pretty sure I heard wrong. Because if it's very unlikely for the two of us to meet randomly on the bus the same day as the bike incident this morning—what are the odds that his name is so similar to mine?

"How do you spell that?" I ask—which is maybe not the usual answer when someone says their name but is a very good way to find out if I heard him correctly.

He's still smiling, which not everyone does after hearing an answer they weren't expecting. "*G-U-I-L-L-E-R-M-O.*"

"That's amazing," I say.

He laughs. "Amazing when anyone spells it right."

"No, I mean your name. Because my name is Gilah. I spell it *G-I-L-A-H.*"

His eyes get wide.

"You're right," he says. "That is amazing."

He tells me where he goes to school, in case I hadn't just seen him get on the bus. Then he asks me where I go, and I hold my chin high like my brother Asher made me practice in front of the mirror. The name of my school is private information, which I can decide whether or not to share. Sometimes I like to take my time in deciding, because sometimes people treat me differently when they find out where I go to school.

"Brandywine," I say to the boy whose name is like mine. "It's a small school."

Sometimes when you answer a question, you should be careful not to add a new fact at the end. But sometimes it's good to add a new fact either (a) to show that you want to continue the conversation, or (b) because it will stop them from asking other questions that might be none of their business, such as what kind of kids go to my small school. Because people of all ages and all kinds of brains sometimes ask questions that are none of their business.

The boy with the name like mine knows what to do.

"My parents thought my old school was too big," he says. "That's part of why we moved to DC, for my school."

He pauses like he is finished, which means I am supposed to add a relevant-but-not-inappropriate comment or ask a relevant-but-not-inappropriate question. I am trying to think of either one when it turns out he is not finished after all, because he adds, "I think I liked it better when I could be more anonymous. Do the teachers at your school pay, like, a *lot* of attention to everyone?"

I'm watching his lips move while he talks, waiting to see if the next pause means it's my turn. When you're having a conversation, it's important not to answer so fast that they think you're interrupting but also not so slow that they think you're finished being in the conversation.

"Yes!" I say just in time. The person in front of me turns around to look, which could mean I am talking too loud but could also mean they want to join in or that their hat or jacket fell into our seat. Just in case, I finish more softly, "Sometimes they pay *too* much attention."

"Definitely," he nods.

Before he gets off, and before I can change my mind, I quickly take out the invitation I made, from the place in my folder where it is staying very flat.

"Here," I say, handing it to him as he stands up to get off the bus.

He is smiling as he reads it. Like before, he's not smiling to be the kind of jerk who is not worth my time.

But this time I am sure: the boy with the name like mine is smiling to be my friend.

GUILLERMO

BROKEN

My bicycle looks fine,
but it's broken.
The wheel wobbles
like the spinning glass plates
circus acrobats balance on long sticks.

My bicycle looks fine,
but it's broken.
The wheel wobbles
like clay on a pottery wheel,
when you lose control.

My bicycle looks fine,
but it's broken.
The wheel wobbles
like a spinning top
just before
it stops.

ALGEBRA CLASS

PART I

In algebra class
we're learning
rational expressions,
but it all seems
irrational to me.
I'm writing this in the margin
of a worksheet
which looks like
alphabet soup.

The only thing about algebra
that's interesting to me
is the word itself:
algebra.
Algebra comes from
the Arabic language:
it means "the reunion of broken parts,"
which sounds kind of beautiful.

PART II

Almohada, calabaza,
lima, limón,
naranja, jirafa,
ojalá, rincón.

Chisme, fideo,
jarabe, café,
azúcar, arroz,
sorbete, olé!

PART III

Instead of algebra,
what I have done,

is written a poem,
because it's more fun.

The poem I've written
is quite syllabic
made up of Spanish words
drawn from Arabic.

I'm sorry the rest of
this worksheet is blank,
I promise it isn't
some sort of prank.

I prefer to write poems
with all due respects
because I don't know
what in the world equals x.

DETENTION

PART I

When the bell rang,
the students funneled themselves
out the doorway
one by one
to freedom,
but Mr. Whitaker cleared his throat,
adjusted his yellow bow tie,
and said in his deep, rumbling voice,
"Mr. Alas, see me at lunch, please."
So at lunch, I got my tray:
grilled cheese, tomato soup, apple slices,
and a carton of milk,
and I went back to Room 233,
where Mr. Whitaker was sitting at his desk,
eating leftover spaghetti
from a plastic container,
his bald brown head
shining beneath the fluorescent lights.

"Sit," he said
without looking up
and pointed to the desk
directly in front of his.

I sat, but didn't eat much,
because when I opened my milk,
it smelled sour,
which made me feel
not so hungry anymore.

PART II

Finally,
Mr. Whitaker wiped his mouth
on a napkin,
sighed,
and held up my paper.

"Mr. Alas," he said.
"What class is this?"

"Eighth grade math," I said.

He poked at my poems

with a pen

peppering them

with red dots.

"Save this for creative writing class, Mr. Alas."

"Yes, sir," I said.

"And if you don't understand the material,

I'm here at lunch, and there's tutoring

after school on Thursdays."

"Yes, sir," I said again.

Mr. Whitaker stared at me,

like my parents do,

waiting to make sure

the words he said,

seeped into my head,

like water

soaking into soil.

When the bell rang,
Mr. Whitaker said I could go
so I gathered my things,
but before I reached the door,
his voice pulled me back,
"Mr. Alas,"
he pushed a pink-colored paper
into my hands.
"I showed your poems
to Ms. Díaz, your English teacher.
She thinks
this might be something
you'd be interested in."

The students for the next class
push past me
into the classroom.
I look at the pink paper
with the words
POETRY CONTEST
at the top.

Mr. Whitaker just nods,
then turns toward the board
to scratch equations in chalk
onto the dark green surface.

WATERCOLOR

In art class,
the teacher says
we'll be painting
with watercolors.

As instructed,
I use a pencil
to make a light sketch
on the thick, textured paper
before I dip my brush
into the water
and begin to paint.

I paint a place much different than DC.
I paint a place
that is simple, and quiet,
like where my grandparents live in West Virginia.
I paint a place
of green mountains, and blue sky,

a place one could ride a bicycle

and not get hit by a bus.

"Be careful not to use too much water,"

the teacher says,

her many bracelets jingling

as she walks past my table.

But it's too late.

My mountains are growing

taller

and

wider

green becoming blue

and blue becoming green

until the sky

has become mountains

and the mountains have become

sky.

NICKNAMES/APODOS

PART I

When I get on the bus
the girl from this morning
is sitting there
in the same seat
in a halo of sunshine
and I wonder for a minute
if she's been riding the bus around all day
or if she's a saint.

I tell her my name is Guillermo,
but I don't tell her
all my nicknames
like Memo, Mo-mo, Zancudito, Capitán, Yum Yum Pollo or
Junior.

My mom says,
"The more apodos you have,
the more loved you are,"

and I like that each name
has a little story
about what makes you
you.

Memo
is what a lot of people
call me
because that's
the short version
of my name.

Mo-mo
is what my little sister
calls me
because when she was a baby
she couldn't say
Guillermo.

Zancudito
is what my abuela, Mamá Tomasa
used to call me

because I'd zoom around the room
like a mosquito
bugging her
when she tried to sew
or watch TV.

Capitán
is what my Tío Ulises
calls me
because Captain America
was my Halloween costume
three years in a row.

Yum Yum Pollo
is what my primos Alex, Lucas, Bernardo, and Nelson
call me
because that's who sponsored my soccer team one year
and that's what was printed across the back of my jersey
in the place where my surname ALAS should have been.

Junior

is what my prima Mayra

calls me

because her mother,

my Tía Carolina,

says I look like

a younger version of my father

even though everyone agrees,

I have my mother's smile.

PART II

I wonder if Gilah

has any nicknames.

Maybe,

if we become friends

I can give her one.

PART III

I asked Gilah
if she liked the nickname
Lala or Gilita
but instead of picking one
she shook her head
and said,
"Just Gilah."

GILAH

LESSON

At home, I hurry up and grab an apple and a cheese stick. There is so much about my life I can't control, but vitamins and protein are two of the things I can.

I'm a little sorry that I don't still have my invitation I made, because I would like to hang it up next to the real invitation at home where my family could notice how mine is better. But then I remember that the reason I don't have it is that the boy in the coat—Guillermo, with the two *L*'s that sound like *Y*—has it. He is officially invited to my bat mitzvah.

I'm pretty sure this wasn't how we learned to invite people in social learning class. But it worked anyway. He is invited. The hardest thing about rules is that sometimes you can follow all the rules A-plus-one-hundred-percent and things still go wrong— then other times you can forget all the rules completely and things still turn out fine.

Maybe growing up is more about learning *not* to follow rules that weren't all that great to begin with.

At four o'clock I run down the street to the synagogue and upstairs to the library, where my Hebrew tutor, Josh, is waiting for me.

Some things about Josh, my bat mitzvah tutor, are that (a) he graduated from the Curtis Institute of Music, which is a school in Philadelphia for people who are already really good at music before they even arrive, and (b) when he tells you where he went to school, he'll make it sound like not a big deal, like anyone who tries hard enough can just walk in and get a music degree there. Also (c), an interesting thing that happened to him while he was in Philadelphia going to music school was that he decided to become Jewish, which is not a decision that many African-American people who grew up singing in the choir at their Baptist church decide. Something Josh and I have in common is that sometimes people are surprised by us for just being ourselves, even though there is no reason to be. Anyway, now he is working part-time as a bar and bat mitzvah tutor and also teaching Hebrew School while he is working on applications for more school so he can someday be a cantor. (Not everyone knows that synagogues often have different people leading the singing parts of a service—the cantors—and the talking parts of a service, the rabbis.)

"Hey, Gilah, how's it going?" he asks, like always.

"Good," I answer, like always, because I know that isn't lying now, even when things aren't good. It's called small talk, and it's very important to some people to help them feel comfortable in a conversation, like wading into the sloped entry at Francis Pool rather than jumping right into the deep end. And if some people find small talk very important, I shouldn't make fun of it if I don't want people making fun of things that are important to me. That is a rule that I wish other people understood better.

"All right, you ready for today? We're on the home stretch!"

Home stretch is not small talk; it's an idiom, which is a phrase that doesn't mean what the individual words would mean on their own. This idiom is from baseball, and it's talking about the distance a runner has to travel from third base to home plate to score a run. I know Josh is being nice and that getting ready for a bat or bar mitzvah is stressful for everyone—but being on the home stretch still feels like there's a long way to go.

We go over a few of the blessings, to limber up my mouth muscles, he says, and then he pulls out the section where I'll read from the Torah about Joseph and his coat with all the colors.

Here is what the word for *colors* looks like in the Torah:

צְבָעִים

The words in the Torah are missing the little lines and dots underneath that do the same thing as vowels in English. I used to think that sounded like my life: I imagined that other people have the letters *and* the vowel sounds to figure out what they're supposed to say, but my copy was missing the vowel sounds. Some people think that means something's wrong with me—but if the Torah, the holiest book in our whole entire religion, is missing the vowel sounds too, I think that proves that "harder to read" does not equal "broken."

And being friends with Guillermo makes me realize that maybe everyone wonders if they're missing something, sometimes.

This time, when I practice reading out loud, there is an actual coat of many colors in my mind, and it belongs to Guillermo. I picture him in the front row of the synagogue during my bat mitzvah, even though I don't know if he'll sit there for real, and I picture myself standing on the bimah singing about his coat.

It's the first time I sing my whole portion from the Torah perfectly from beginning to end.

DANCE

Every night I practice my Torah portion, which I'll read in synagogue the morning of my bat mitzvah, and I also practice my dance moves for the party at night.

These things are different but a little bit the same. The Hebrew letters are thick in some places, thin in others. Sometimes the pieces connect, like an arm or leg branching off for a kick, and other times there are loose little semi-lines hanging off by themselves, like they are in the middle of flipping upside down. Like they are breakdancing.

When I go downstairs to our basement after dinner, here are some of the things that are there:

- hammock
- glider swing
- trampoline
- giant exercise ball

But the best thing in our basement is the floor mat. Originally we got it for gymnastics, but the floor mat is super-important this year. That's because the tutoring sessions with Josh are only one kind of preparation for a bat mitzvah. The other kind is the dancing.

At my brother Asher's bar mitzvah, a whole bunch of his friends made a circle around me and clapped while I busted out the moves, but later Asher got mad at some of them for being jerks who were not worth either of our time.

This time will be different, though: I was just a beginner then, and I've been practicing a lot, including with hand weights, plus I'm older, so I can do a lot more. And also this time it is *my* bat mitzvah.

I'm down there on the floor mat, windmilling, and I think what I really need is the music, so I set up the speakers on my phone. I guess it's louder than I realized, because pretty soon Miri is on the steps yelling over the music that she HAS TO DO HOMEWORK because she is in MIDDLE SCHOOL now.

"SO DO HOMEWORK!" I yell back over the music.

"I CAN'T WITH YOUR MUSIC!" she yells.

"IT'S FOR MY BAT MITZVAH!" I yell back.

Miri doesn't yell back right away. Instead, she says, "You're not doing that at your bat mitzvah."

My mom is on the steps now too. "Gilah, the music is pretty loud."

That's true, of course, but loud isn't always a problem: if there was any doubt about that before, I learned that for sure that day on the bus. Plus, since my mom and I agree that the music is loud, then maybe if I don't turn it down she'll just think I didn't hear her.

Miri says, "Mom, tell her. Kids will laugh if she dances like that. Just like they did at Asher's."

"They weren't laughing!" I say.

First of all, Miri was little at Asher's bar mitzvah, and she might not remember the crowd of older boys, clapping and stomping their feet while I showed off my moves.

I remember Asher's friends in a circle, or really just the feet of Asher's friends, wearing mismatched silly socks for fun, which is allowed at a bar mitzvah.

And however Miri thinks people reacted or didn't react to my moves from three years ago, she has no idea how people will react to what I've got planned.

"Miri, relax," my mom says.

"I'm just trying to help!" Miri answers.

"Stop helping!" I say, at the same time my mom says, "The kids in her class know how to be nice to each other," which is true, I guess, even though it should also be true for the kids in Asher's class. Also, knowing how to be nice isn't the same as being nice. But I guess it's enough for Miri to stomp back upstairs.

"Gilah," my mom says. Then she pantomimes turning a knob, which makes no sense because phones don't have knobs, and she says, "Quieter!"

So I turn the sound down just a drop, then wait a few seconds before turning it back up. After all, my mom didn't say how long I had to keep it turned down.

I'm windmilling, which means I am basically a rotating Hebrew letter lah-med, and in my head I finish my routine in a perfect backflip, which—unlike my little sister, who is an amazing gymnast—I currently can't do. In my head, the kids from my class are standing in a circle around me, clapping and cheering me on, and Guillermo is clapping and cheering with everyone else.

I wonder if Guillermo knows how to breakdance. Not like someone who has been studying and practicing, of course, but maybe he might want to make up a poem with his body sometime instead of writing down words. I wonder if I should tell him to bring sweatpants, in case he wants to take off the many-colored coat and just dance.

CAR RIDE

Tuesdays I have therapy at a place in Virginia so far away that the area code changes from 703—which are the parts of Virginia right over the bridge from the monuments and even as far as Tysons Corner Mall—to 540, which is for horseback-riding and the Shenandoah Valley. Zip codes change all the time, but going two area codes away means we pass four Giant supermarkets between our house and the therapy place. Also three Shell gas stations, five Exxons, and four BPs. We also pass five Starbucks coffee places if you count the one at the end of the shopping center where my therapy is, which technically we don't pass on the way. Proportions are important in geometry and in art but also in my mom's coffee order: the stressfulness of her day is proportional to the fanciness of her coffee drink, which means that more stress in her life equals more complicated instructions to the barista.

In the car, she reminds me, "My new job is a flexible job, which means I can still come to your school if you need me. Or if Asher or Miri needs me," she adds.

The new job is at an organization, which is like a company except it usually pays less, and she used to do pretty much the same job for a different organization before Miri was born, except the other organization gave her an office with a door, and at this organization she has a cubicle.

In some ways a cubicle might be better than an office, because you can use thumbtacks to put whatever you want all over the fabric-covered walls, but in an office someone might yell at you if you make holes in the wall or use tape that can peel off the paint.

I think of offering some of my special gold thumbtacks. But she is merging into traffic, so I wait a minute, and by then I am not actually sure I want to share my special gold thumbtacks, so I keep quiet. Maybe part of being almost a grown-up is deciding what I get to keep just for me.

IHOP

On the ride to my therapy in Virginia, Miri keeps accidentally kicking my seat from behind because she is not paying attention due to being upset because her ankle hurts. Although you would think she'd notice that the kicking is making her ankle hurt worse.

"Stop kicking," I tell her.

"I'm not kicking," she says.

"I know when someone's kicking."

"That's enough, Mir," says my mom.

Miri lets out a low sigh and says, "It *is*," under her breath, and I guess I kind of agree with her because when she kicks my seat again, I yell, "STOP KICKING MY SEAT!"

And my mom yells, "Miri, I said that's enough!"

Which is when I notice we've been stopped in traffic in front of the same shopping center for a long time, and the traffic looks really bad up ahead, and I'm supposed to take my meds with a meal at the exact same time every day.

When you're stuck in the middle of a long line of cars, you can't tell where it ends—the next exit or all the way back to our house in DC or somewhere even farther. Or even if it never ends at all.

"Are you guys hungry?" my mom asks. "There's an IHOP in there. We could stop for dinner."

"IHOP!" Miri says. One of the things we agree about is the amazingness of IHOP. Our whole family doesn't go together very often because Asher once threw up at an IHOP on the way home from Bethany Beach, but sometimes it feels like IHOP is the one thing Miri and I have in common.

Up ahead, the blue logo glows like an oasis in the middle of traffic.

Miri stops kicking and I stop yelling, as my mom pulls into the parking lot.

LOST AND FOUND

At IHOP, I always order the same breakfast from the children's menu: eggs—scrambled, two pieces of wheat toast, no bacon because it's not kosher.

It used to upset me how the menu uses 'N instead of *and*, for Rise 'N Shine, when really if they are going to use an apostrophe in place of a missing letter, they should do 'N'—which looks even worse. Now I just don't look at the menu before I order, which is an example of "letting things go."

There's always a small rack on the table with at least two types of jelly—grape and strawberry, sometimes also peach—and we always ask for extra knives so I can spread strawberry on one piece of toast and grape on the other without mixing them up. (I avoid the peach, which I hate.)

But tonight there's only strawberry and peach.

"Are you having your usual?" my mom asks.

"There's no grape jelly," I point out.

"So use the strawberry," Miri says.

"I like both!"

"We'll ask her to bring the grape," my mom offers.

The waitress has blonde hair that is streaked in rainbow colors. Her name tag says "DESTINY," which maybe has something to do with why her head looks like a rainbow. Or maybe her hair has nothing to do with her name at all, like how *Gilah* means joy but I'm not obligated to wear smiley faces all the time.

Miri asks DESTINY for a Belgian waffle: something Miri and I have in common is that we both order something other than pancakes at the International House of Pancakes.

My mom orders pumpkin spice pancakes, and then she says, "Gilah?" so I know it's my turn.

"Hi," I say, because it's almost always OK to say hi to a restaurant server, although I don't know whether it's OK to use DESTINY's first name which I learned from her name tag, because what if she forgot she had it on and found it weird that I knew her name? "Could I please have the eggs—scrambled, wheat toast, no bacon, from the children's menu and two extra knives?"

"Extra knives?" DESTINY asks.

"Yes," my mom says. "Two extra knives."

"I'll see what I can do," says DESTINY.

"Thank you," says my mom. "And if you could please bring over some grape jelly when you get a chance."

"OK," says DESTINY. "But I don't know if she can still order from the kids."

"I'll pay for the adult size," my mom offers. "If you could just arrange it like from the children's menu—"

"I'll see what I can do," DESTINY says again, backing up from our table and bumping into an empty table behind her.

When DESTINY comes back, she has the extra knives, and a handful of jelly packets. But my plate has four pieces of toast on it, not two, and hash browns that I didn't even order.

"We'll fix it," my mom whispers, as DESTINY dumps the jelly packets on the table.

Sometimes I wish my mom were a little less focused on fixing things. In this case, she fixes the plate but can't fix the fact that the jelly that has just been dumped on our table is more of the strawberry and peach that we already had.

"There's still no grape jelly!" I yell.

"I'm going to wait in the car," says Miri.

Out of the corner of my eye, I see DESTINY wiping the table of a family that has just left.

Just past where her arm is wiping back and forth, slowly across the table, are packets of jelly: three types neatly stacked, all with different-colored lids.

I wait for DESTINY to finish wiping. Then, when my mom looks down at her pancakes, I slide myself out of our booth. By the time she breathes out again, I'm five feet away, at the other table.

I'm reaching for the grape jelly to bring back to our table when, through the crack between the table and the wall, I notice something unexpectedly shiny down below.

Before I can think about it too hard, I slide down onto the floor, and when I slide back up, I am holding a shiny earring.

The rule is that if you find something that doesn't belong to you, you should try to help it get back to whoever it belongs to if it is something that a person might want back.

At IHOP, the best place to do that is at the front counter.

"Excuse me," I ask, "is there a lost and found?"

Possibly I am a little loud, but that's because I'm not as close to the counter as I would be if I weren't also watching the table, making sure DESTINY or someone else doesn't swoop in to collect my plate, thinking I'm finished with dinner, faster than my mom can stop them.

Watching the table is even more important after my mom is suddenly next to me, asking, "Gilah, what did you lose?"

I want to tell her that we're now both in danger of losing our dinner plates, along with the to-go box holding Miri's dinner, but first I need to clarify that I am participating in a lost and found as a finder.

"Nothing!" I say, unfolding my hand to show her the earring. "I found this under that other table."

By then, the person at the counter is yelling into the kitchen, definitely not modulating her voice, "Did anyone lose an earring?"

And then DESTINY is there, touching her empty earlobe as she looks around frantically.

"Ohmigod, ohmigod, thank you," she's saying, before she even knows who she's thanking. I think she's maybe just expecting the earring to float by her in the air or something.

When I hold out my hand, she picks it up delicately and says, "Ohmigod, thank you," again, then adds, "They're from my boyfriend, he gave these to me for my birthday."

DESTINY doesn't look at my face to notice whether I'm the same person who needed extra spreading knives.

"No problem," I say.

My eggs and toast are still safely on our table, and my mom's pancakes are too, even though she stands by the counter a minute longer, looking back and forth from me to DESTINY and back again. DESTINY already has the earring back in her ear, and she's smiling.

I smile too, as I look at the jelly arrangement on the other table, which is the whole reason I found the missing earring. If it weren't for me, that earring might have been vacuumed up, maybe even by DESTINY herself, after the restaurant had closed.

I bring some grape jelly with me when I slide back into our booth.

My mom is smiling too. "I'm sorry I jumped to conclusions," she says. "You really helped someone out."

Finally, I spread strawberry jelly on one piece of toast and grape jelly on another. I take alternating bites to let my whole mouth enjoy that celebration.

GUILLERMO

FLU

PART I

I arrive home
and she says, "Achoo!"
Mom tells me my sister
has gotten the flu.

I promise to stay
far, far away
for a few days
so I won't catch it too.

PART II

Araceli usually
Races to greet me
Araceli usually
Comes barging into my room, without knocking
Especially when she has something exciting to show me
Like a roly-poly curled like a tiny insect armadillo, or an
Igloo made from sugar cubes.

I usually get annoyed, but
Seeing her on the sofa

Sleepy and quiet
I sort of miss her nonsensical knock-knock jokes.
Cousins and siblings, I've come to realize, are both
Kind of like built-in friends.

PART III

That igloo
she once made

from sugar cubes

got left out in the rain

because Araceli

wanted to experiment

and see if ants

would move into it

(even though I told her

they would probably eat it).

But before the ants got a chance,

the rain disintegrated the sugar cubes

to nothing,

which my mother said

was still an interesting experiment

but that didn't stop Araceli

from crying for days.

My mother told her

she could build another igloo,

but Araceli refused

and said it wouldn't be the same

as the one she left out in the rain.

Sometimes that's how I feel
about trying to build new friendships at school,
when what I want
are the old friendships
I left behind.

PAPER CUT

When I go up to my room,
to do my homework,
I slice my finger
on the edge of a page.

It looks insignificant,
but hurts a lot, and
I know it will take
quite a while to heal.

Maybe sometimes
hurting inside
is like that too.

PARAKEETS IN THE CORNFIELD

It's almost dinnertime,

and I haven't figured out

how to tell my parents

what happened to my bicycle,

but I need to tell them,

so they can give me money

to get the tire fixed.

I need to tell them,

but maybe not the whole story,

maybe not the part

about the bus knocking me down.

But when I get close to the kitchen,

I hear low voices,

my parents are talking,

so I wait

in the hallway,

out of sight.

My mother is talking about
the cost of the doctor visit for my sister,
saying,
"If I don't go back to work,
what will we do for insurance?"

And my father is talking about
the rising cost of ingredients at the bakery,
saying,
"But the plan was for you to help get the bakery going the
first year,
I can't afford employees right now."

And
they both sound
frustrated.

My mother wipes her hands on a rag
and sighs toward the ceiling,
as if asking the universe to ease up.
My father is drumming a finger
against the countertop

and it sounds like a steady, leaking faucet.
They both look
tired.

My mother starts to speak again,
but my father clears his throat,
and says, "Hay pericos en la milpa,"
which means, "There's parakeets in the cornfield,"
but he doesn't mean a real parakeet in a real cornfield,
he means me, sitting here in the hallway, listening.
It's his way of telling my mother
they should talk about it later.

I think it's not a good time to ask them for money,
or tell them what happened to my bicycle.
This parakeet isn't making a peep.

ALL I HAVE

I shake my piggy bank,
which isn't a piggy,
but an empty coffee can.

A quarter pings,
then rolls,
around the inside.
Twenty-five cents is all I have.

I ask the neighbors
if I can walk their dogs.
Everyone says, "No thanks," or
"We already have a dog walker,"
or "Can you come around noon?"
which is when I'm at school,
so I can't.

Matthew and Khalil
who live next door
say I can walk their cat,

but Miss Mochi
plops down and rolls
on the sidewalk,
tries to bite the leash
in her tiny, sharp teeth
and meows
low and long
with her tail flicking
when I try to nudge her.

Matthew and Khalil
give me a dollar.

A dollar twenty-five is all I have.

On Saturday
I hold a yard sale.
Because I don't have much,
not many people stop by.
A little boy buys a few of my
Panini fútbol stickers.

A dollar fifty is all I have.

On Sunday
I ask everyone on my street
if I can rake their leaves.
One white-haired lady hires me.

Six dollars and fifty cents is all I have.

On Monday
at school
I find a dime on the dusty floor
near the cafeteria,
and a penny
on the sidewalk.

Six dollars and sixty-one cents is all I have.

Six dollars and sixty-one cents
is probably not enough
to get my bicycle fixed.

BRUNO'S BICYCLES & REPAIR

PART I

At Bruno's Bicycles & Repair
bicycles hang all over the walls
and upside down from the ceiling,
like the airplanes
at the Air & Space Museum.

There are
bicycles for adults and children;
mountain bikes and city bikes;
bicycles low to the ground
with seats you can relax into;
tall, skinny racing bikes;
BMX bikes for stunts;
bicycles with baskets on the front;
bicycles with racks on the back;
bicycles with bells that chime;
bicycles with horns that honk;
bicycles with lights that flash;

bicycles with handlebar streamers;

bicycles with orange flags and saddlebags;

bicycle antiques with long seats;

and a tandem bicycle for two.

There are as many types of bicycles

as there are types of people.

But that reminds me of the one thing

I don't see here in this shop—people.

Or rather, one person in particular:

Bruno.

PART II

Beyond the counter

there's a doorway to a garage

and the sound of a wrench

dropping on the cement floor.

"Hello?"

I lean my bike against the counter.

"May I speak to Bruno, please?"

"You can, but he probably won't say anything back,"
a man with blond hair tied into a bun and tattooed arms appears.
"I'm Ryan. That there's Bruno," he points with a screwdriver
to a black and white French bulldog
asleep in the front window.

"You trying to upgrade this beater?"
he looks down at my bike.

"I want to fix it," I say.

Ryan sets the screwdriver on the counter,
and takes my bike by the handlebars.
He whistles low.
"This get hit by the Metro or something?"
"Something like that," I mumble,
and feel the tips of my ears
go hot.

Ryan kneels down. "You might need a new rim.
Can't say for sure without taking it off and putting it
on the stand,

but pretty sure I can't true this."

"How much will a new rim cost?"
"One forty," Ryan says. "At least."
"A dollar and forty cents?"
My hand finds the crumpled bills
tucked into the dark corner of my
father's coat pocket.

"No, a hundred and forty," Ryan frowns.
"For that amount, you may want to just get a new bike."

I don't have a hundred and forty dollars,
and I don't want a new bike,
I want this one
because I don't want my parents to ask
what happened to my old bike,
and besides,
this one is
special,
but when I tell Ryan
he just rubs his chin,

and insists I leave my bike with him

(and Bruno)

anyway.

"Listen, write down your name and number.

I'll give you an estimate before I do anything to it,

then we can go from there."

I write down my name

but not my phone number

because I don't want Ryan

to call my house

or my parents will find out.

"I don't have a phone number," I say.

"I mean, I don't have my own phone number."

Ryan looks confused, and then he smiles

like he understands

without me explaining.

"No problem. Just come back next Friday

to check on your bike.

Me and Bruno will be here. Won't we, Bruno?"

Bruno opens his eyes, and tilts his head

at the mention of his name.

I don't see the point of leaving it with Ryan,

because I can't afford the repairs,

but in this condition,

there's no point in taking it back home either.

This is a good place,

to hide it from my parents.

I turn to go.

Just myself and my feet,

and no wheels beneath

me.

PART III

"Hey wait, your name's Guillermo?

Like Guillermo Ochoa

the goalkeeper

for the Mexican soccer team?"

"I guess," I say.

Because Ochoa is a good player,

but I don't want Ryan to get confused
and think I'm from Mexico.

Some people don't understand
I'm American,
even though I was born here,
like my mother.

And some people don't know
where El Salvador is,
or that it even exists.

"You speak Spanish?"
Ryan asks,
and I nod.

"How about this,"
He unrolls a copy of *El Tiempo Latino*
on the countertop.
"If you can help me write an ad to run in this magazine,
I'll charge you only twenty bucks labor,
no matter what the parts cost to fix your bike.

What do you think? Fair deal?"
I don't have twenty dollars,
but twenty dollars is less than a hundred and forty.
Somehow, I will find a way to pay.

We shake on it,
and I help Ryan
write the advertisement,
before I head home.

PART IV

Ryan tells me the information
he wants included,
but gives me what he calls
"creative license"
to write the ad however I think is best.

I like the idea of having a license to be creative,
so next time Mr. Whitaker asks me not to write poems
in the margins of my algebra work,
I could pull out my creative license,

and tell him I'm authorized.

He would inspect my creative license,

compare the photo to my face,

to make sure it's valid, and then he'd hand it back to me,

saying, "Very well then. Carry on."

I decide to write the ad as a poem. It looks like this:

¿Necesitas una bicicleta?

¿O reparaciones?

Bruno's Bicycles & Repair

¡es la bicicletería para campeones!

Translation:

Do you need a bicycle?

Or repairs?

Bruno's Bicycles & Repair

is the bicycle store for champions!

(Except *repairs* and *champions* don't rhyme, so it's not as good in English. Which is what my father says about soccer announcing too.)

BILINGUAL

PART I

Before we moved to DC to start the new bakery
my mom was a bilingual liaison
for a school back in Maryland.

A liaison is kind of like a bridge
connecting two islands.
My mom connected
School Administration Island
with La Isla de Padres Hispanohablantes
(the island of Spanish-speaking parents).

She translated materials,
and interpreted at parent/teacher conferences,
she helped the librarian pick Spanish-language books,
and created displays for Hispanic Heritage month.
But she also advocated
for bilingual education
for all kids,

and all languages,

not just the ones

with Spanish-speaking parents,

because

"Being bilingual is a valuable skill.

Study after study

has proven

bilingual students perform better

in all kinds of things,

including language, math, music,

creative thinking, and problem solving;

they are also more empathetic,

and the world could always use more

empathetic people."

She says this

to almost everyone she meets;

she's said it to the members of the Board of Education,

she's said it to parents at PTA meetings,

she's said it to a politician running for Congress,

she's said it to a stranger at the grocery store

who told us to "speak English because we're in America."

She's said it so often
it's tattooed on my brain,
just as permanent
as the tattoos on Ryan's arms.

Sometimes her enthusiasm for bilingualism
has made me roll my eyes
like when she pretends not to hear me if I respond in English
(even though that's her native language).
But next time she gives her
"Being bilingual is a valuable skill" speech,
I will smile, and she will wonder why.

PART II

Some people are surprised
when they find out
my little sister Araceli
is not bilingual,
at least not as bilingual
as they expect her to be

based on her name,

and what my mom does for a living.

"How is that possible?" they say

and try to find a way

to blame my parents.

Even my abuela, Mamá Tomasa,

would get frustrated

when she'd say something to Araceli,

and Araceli wouldn't understand,

or would pretend that she didn't understand,

if the something Mamá Tomasa said was

something like, "Be quiet," or "You've had enough candy."

When people would ask my mom

"She doesn't speak Spanish?

How is that possible?"

My mom would usually shrug and say,

"You can lead a horse to water,

but you can't make them drink,

and my daughter

is a very stubborn horse."
But sometimes when my mom
was not in the mood for other people's judgment
about her parenting,
or Araceli's language skills,
my mom would say something like,
"What's your heritage?
But you don't speak German, French, or Italian?
That's a shame. There's free language apps,
you should try one."

And the person will usually say that they have tried
to learn another language, but it was too hard,
and then they will realize
the lesson my mom
is trying to teach them,
about judging other people.

BAT MITZVAH

The girl from the bus—Gilah,
gave me an invitation to a bat mitzvah,
except I didn't know what a bat mitzvah was,
so I looked it up on Wikipedia.

I'm a little worried
because I don't have a kippah
which is a little round cap
that all the men wear to bat mitzvahs,
at least that's what I see in pictures.

I'm a little worried
because a bat mitzvah
is kind of like a special birthday party,
and so I'll need a special gift
for Gilah.

I'm a little worried
because I don't speak Hebrew
and I think that is what they speak
at bat mitzvahs.

I'm a little worried
because my family doesn't have bat mitzvahs,
instead we have a fiesta rosa, or quinceañera,
but usually only for girls
when they turn fifteen.

I was in my cousin Mayra's court
at her quince last year
so I know how to waltz
if you waltz at bat mitzvahs,
but I'm not sure.
Wikipedia didn't say.

RSVP

I gave this to Gilah and she smiled:
Thank you for your invitation,
I'll be happy to attend,
and celebrate your special day,
now that you're my friend.

UNCOMFORTABLE QUESTIONS

I haven't known Gilah long
and some days we don't talk much
but that's part of what makes her a good friend.

I don't know many people who let me write
without asking questions like,
"What are you writing?"
Which is an uncomfortable question,
because sometimes I'm not sure
until I'm done writing it.

And if I tell what I'm writing,
most people would ask,
"Can I see it?"
and showing my poems
when they're unfinished
(and sometimes even when they are finished)
feels kind of like that moment at the public pool
between taking your towel off
and getting into the water.

WHEN WE DO TALK

When we do talk
there's no telling what Gilah might say.
(That's another thing
I like about her.)

When we do talk
she makes connections between things
I would never connect.
(Like how a leaf fluttering around on the sidewalk
looks like it's breakdancing.)

GO-GO

PART I

Sometimes when the H4

passes by a convenience store on the corner

there is music playing outside

and I always cross my fingers

that we'll get a red light at the intersection

so I can listen for awhile

to that

bump

BA-bump

bump-DA-dump

that sounds almost

like a heartbeat.

PART II

Gilah sees me listening

for the music in the distance.

The corner store is not yet

in my line of vision
but somehow I can feel
the beat in my bones.

As we pull close to the intersection,
we see people dancing.
Even people who are just walking
walk with a sort of rhythm
like they are too busy getting
from Point A
to Point B
to stop to dance,
but their bodies can't resist
the pulse in the sidewalk
beneath their feet.

PART III

Traffic backs up,
and the bus stops,
with its usual
high-pitched squeal

and *tssssssssssss*
of the brakes.

We are now yards away
from the store on the corner
we can now hear
not just the beat and melody
but a voice in the music.

A man calls to a crowd,
and the crowd responds.
They go back and forth
creating a rhythm that goes:
Let me hear you say,
Heeeeey—eyyy-yaaaay
(Heeeey—eyyy-yaaaay)
Now, let me hear you go,
Whooooa—oooh-ooh-oh
(Whooooa—oooh-ooh-oh)
A little bit louder now.
Heeeeey—eyyy-yaaaay
(Heeeey—eyyy-yaaaay)

I can't hear you!
Whooooa—oooh-ooh-oh
(Whooooa—oooh-ooh-oh)

The beat continues,
but the melody changes
one song becomes another
blending together
like watercolor paints
blue into green,
green into blue.

PART IV

I ask Gilah,
"Can you open the window please?"
but she stares out at the street,
like I've said nothing at all.

I tell her it'll only be for a minute,
that I'm just trying to hear something better,
but instead of answering me

she starts to get upset.
Pink splotches bloom on her cheeks
like the cherry blossoms I saw
near the Jefferson Memorial
when my family visited
the National Mall last April,
like we used to do
before we lived here.

"Never mind," I say,
trying not to sound too mad
as we pass through the intersection,
and down the street,
leaving the music behind.

GILAH

OPENING

Sometimes the question somebody asks is not actually what they want to know, if they even want to know anything at all.

For instance, when a math teacher asks, "Can you solve a two-variable equation in algebra?" they actually want to know what you can do.

But when someone asks, "Can you believe this weather?" they just want you to agree that it's very cold or hot or rainy or whatever, because the weather is a safe topic of conversation.

And when Guillermo says, "Can you open the window please?" the "please" is a verbal cue that he would like me to do something.

When answering a question, it is polite to respond quickly. Sometimes you can get extra time to answer if you say something like, "Let me check and get back to you." But that only works for some kinds of questions, and "Can you open the window please?" is not that kind.

The reason I need more time is because of a sticker above my head, which is mostly worn off, so a not very experienced bus rider like Guillermo would not know what it says. There are stickers like this on other windows, but those are mostly blocked by people's heads. Those stickers say what this sticker used to say: When A/C is on please keep windows closed for passenger comfort.

A/C stands for *air conditioner*, even though there is no slash mark or other punctuation in *air conditioner*. I am not under a vent, so it is hard to be a hundred percent sure, but it is October, which is not typically a month when air conditioning is needed in the northern hemisphere, which includes Washington, DC.

Sometimes directions rely on intuition instead of spelling out every single possible situation, which would make the sticker so big it blocks the whole window. For example, if it is raining or there is a blizzard, passengers would also be more comfortable with the window closed, even if the A/C is not on.

Also, the sticker says "passenger" instead of "passengers"—so maybe the comfort of just one passenger is enough to consider when making the decision about the window.

In which case, Guillermo is a passenger.

He wants to hear the go-go music outside.

This is an example of the "rules" not really helping to figure out the best thing to do: Guillermo getting something he wants may or may not help with the comfort of other passengers.

But maybe a passenger who isn't yet comfortable with go-go music will turn out to love it—so opening the window will help with their comfort too.

I reach for the red lever to open the window.

But the go-go music is behind us now, and Guillermo is already off the bus.

GUILLERMO

THE WINDOW

PART I

The next day
as we approach the corner store with the music
Gilah opens the window.

PART II

"That's go-go,"
Gilah says
after the beat fades
and she closes the window.

I look at her with the question
on my face:
What's go-go?

"The music you wanted to hear,"
she says.
"That's go-go.

It's a sub-genre of funk,
mixed with R&B
that was created in DC,
back in the 70s
before my parents were even born."

When I ask Gilah,
"How do you know all this?"
She shrugs and says,
"It's good music for breakdancing,"
as if that answers my question.

We sit quietly for a few minutes,
past Georgia Avenue Northwest all the way to
Children's Hospital.

"Gilah, do you breakdance?"
I finally ask.
She keeps her forehead
pressed against the window,
so that her warm breath fogs the cold glass
when she says,
"Yes."

HOW GO-GO WAS INVENTED

To keep people
from leaving the dance floor
a man named Chuck Brown,
the godfather of go-go music,
and his band
started playing music
between the songs,
one song
flowing into the next,
and it ended up
that even more than the songs
that came before or after,
people liked
those in-between parts
best.

DETOUR AHEAD

The big orange sign
warns of a detour ahead
the bus takes a turn
I've never been down this road
Sometimes life is like that too

SIGH

Today I didn't feel like writing.
Sometimes that happens.
So I decided to people watch
out the window.
When we passed by a bicyclist
I must have sighed a little because
Gilah studied my face
then asked if it was
a frustrated sigh,
a happy sigh,
a tired sigh,
a sigh of relief,
or if I was having trouble breathing,
which made me smile,
because that was a very Gilah thing to say.

WORTH

I told Gilah I'm a little frustrated
about my bicycle
because I don't have enough
to pay for the repairs.
I hadn't mentioned it
because I didn't want her to think
I was asking her for money
or that my family is
"economically disadvantaged"
as my mom says,
even though we kind of are right now.
But don't say that in front of my father
because he'll quote Santo Romero,
a saint from El Salvador
admired by many
as a defender of the poor
who said things like,
"El hombre no vale
por lo que tiene,
sino por lo que es."

Or in English,

"Man is not worth

what he has,

but what he is."

Which means

it's not about the things you own,

but who you are as a person,

and that's true,

but it doesn't make me feel better

about not having my bicycle.

GILAH

CATASTROPHE

"NOOOOOOO!"

That is the sound of my sister Miri screaming, which is much louder than you might imagine based on the size of her lungs. (A lot of people mix up volume-as-in-loudness with volume-as-in-capacity, which doesn't make sense if they notice that music can still be really loud on old-fashioned records or CDs.)

When I was little, Miri and I were so close that part of my brain used to think we were the same person. When she screamed—such as if I knocked my cereal bowl into her lap when she was wearing a new outfit, or if I borrowed one of her special Magic Markers because the regular Magic Markers didn't have a special color I needed, such as teal—my brain told my body to react the same way as if I was the one screaming: find a place where I felt safe, then curl up in a ball and rock back and forth until I was sure everything was OK.

That changed after Miri hurt herself one time, tripping over a shoe that I may or may not have left on the stairs. She was bleeding and screaming, and I waited for my body to magically transport me to the nearest safe space, but that didn't happen because of course we are different people. Which I guess is mostly a good thing, even if it seemed like we liked each other better when we were younger.

Now when Miri screams, I do not curl up as if I am the one screaming. If I'm in a different room but near a computer, I sometimes turn on a sound-wave app that lets you track the sound waves of a scream. If I'm in the same room as the scream but am not the person being screamed at, I sometimes put on headphones to avoid being overstimulated.

This time I am not near a computer but I am also not near headphones, because I left them in my backpack, which is on a hook in the mudroom. To walk down the hall to my backpack, I have to pass Miri and my mother, who in this case is the person being screamed at.

My mom is saying, "Sweetie, we all do a lot to get you to as many of these events as possible, but you can't miss your sister's bat mitzvah for a gymnastics meet."

I like how my mom said "we all," reminding Miri that every member of our family has adjusted their schedule for Miri's gymnastics at one time or another.

In general, the older a person is, the more likely he or she has done something to become famous. That's just because of math, because the only people who are famous as kids are the people who did something when they were really young, but famous older people includes all of those people plus the ones who did something famous-making when they got older. This logic is imperfect because it doesn't include: (1) kids who became famous by being related to a famous older person and (2) people who were famous a long time ago but everyone has forgotten.

Still, the logic is true enough that if I asked you to guess the most famous member of my family, you probably would not guess my younger sister Miri. She is not the kind of famous where people stop her in the grocery store and demand her autograph, though she would probably enjoy that. She is the kind of famous where she qualified as a Junior Olympic gymnast a few years ago and was all set to fly to Orlando even though she would have had to compete on Shabbat, but then she tore a ligament at Asher's bar mitzvah and had to rest her leg.

I learned practically a whole page of rules as a result of that experience, such as:

• The rule about not competing on Shabbat is different if you qualify as a Junior Olympic gymnast.

• People who hurt themselves and have to miss something they were looking forward to don't like it if you ask them if this is related to the rule above.

• More girls than boys do gymnastics, but more boys than girls do breakdancing. This is not a rule but is a fact. Another fact is that gymnastics and breakdancing are mostly distinguished by the clothes and the music. I, for one, am hoping that breakdancing gets as much respect as gymnastics in the sports world after it is finally added to the Olympics in 2024. And if they start to get equal respect in the sports world, they'll definitely get equal respect in my house.

And maybe the most important rule:

• If someone has no chance of qualifying for something—for example, me qualifying for Miss America, which is mostly based on skinniness and remembering to smile at illogical times—

there is much less disappointment than when someone *almost* qualifies for something, such as Miri in the Junior Olympics.

• And a corollary to this rule, which means a rule that attaches itself onto the first one: the amount of resentment over being told you can't try again goes up the closer you came the first time. That is something Miri and I have in common: we both get frustrated when other people think we can't do something or tell us we can't try again.

Which is why it's a really, really, really big problem for Miri that the qualifying meet is on the same day as my bat mitzvah.

RESCUE

Miri refuses to eat dinner. She doesn't come down to the basement to *thump-thump-thump* her roundoffs, so I decide to wait in the hallway outside her room. Because I have big news she will want to know, and people do not appreciate tapping on their door, even to announce big news. But she will have to come to the hallway eventually when she needs to use the bathroom.

I am holding an iPad that has one window open to Miri's big news that she doesn't know about yet, and one window to a YouTube video where I am learning about breakdancing with the sound off.

It would be much better with the sound on, so I could hear the explanations of what they're doing, but I did not bring my headphones into the hall, so I now have a dilemma about whether to go get them and risk missing Miri's trip to the bathroom or listen without the headphones (which will annoy Miri more than she is already annoyed) or keep watching with the sound off, which will annoy me.

If I turn the sound on, Miri might be annoyed enough to come to the hallway, which would mean I'd no longer need to wait for her to use the bathroom. Plus, when she comes out, she'll soon be un-annoyed because I will (a) turn off the sound and (b) share the big news.

I turn on the sound. And right on cue, Miri opens her door! People are so much easier when they are predictable.

"Quiet!" she announces. "Some of us have homework and a headache!"

"You might be dehydrated," I offer, remembering that she didn't eat dinner and has not needed to use the bathroom.

"You might need to turn the sound off on your breakdancing video!"

I reach for the iPad but then have to stand in her doorway so she doesn't think the conversation is over.

"Wait!" I say. "There's big news!"

"About breakdancing?"

"No!" I say. "Gymnastics!" I am so happy to have identified news on a topic of interest to Miri.

"Leave me alone!"

"No!" I say again, quickly navigating off YouTube even though I'll probably have to start the video over again from the beginning.

"Look!" I shove the iPad on the gymnastics screen where she can see it and not close the door on it.

"That is not big news," she says. "The big news is that I have to miss the biggest day of my life due to *your* bat mitzvah. Just like you tripped me at Asher's bar mitzvah so I had to miss that meet too!"

"I didn't trip you!" I yell. What happened was that I was breakdancing and Asher's friends were stomping and clapping, and Miri for some unknown reason tried to work her way into the middle of the circle, which caused us to get tangled up in each other.

As I shove my way into Miri's doorway, I accidentally land inside her room.

"Get out of my room!" she yells.

Her room is a mess, piles of clothes and old homework papers. I can't remember the last time I was in here.

Quickly I yell the most important point, "You can do it a different day!"

"What do you mean, a different day? That's not how the world works!"

"But it is!" I love being right about something that will make Miri happy, if she can only be quiet long enough for me to tell her. "The world works in regions! And the other regions have their meets on different days!"

Miri is quiet, which I take as a very good sign. In my calmest voice I say, "I know how the world works because I know how to read, and the website does not say you can only compete in the qualifying match for the region where you live."

My dad comes halfway up the stairs, holding his phone.

"Well, that was the world's quickest answer," he said.

What was?

"Gilah is right," he says. "If we take you up to Baltimore, you could qualify the week after the bat mitzvah."

Miri doesn't say anything but looks at the screen on my dad's phone, which has the exact same information I was trying to show her on the iPad, only with smaller print.

"I have to ask my coach," she says.

"And thank your sister," my dad whisper-says, which is called a stage whisper.

Miri rolls her eyes.

"Thank you," she says. Then, after my dad has left the room, she adds, under her breath, "Even though your bat mitzvah was what caused the problem to start with."

Which is not exactly a total thank you, but I'm smiling so big I don't care. Downstairs, my dad has his calendar app open and is showing my mom how all of our schedules will work out after all.

I wait for him to finish talking and then I say, "There's never just one way to do things, isn't that what you taught me? If you can't learn something one way, you learn it a different way, right? If there's ice on Porter Street, the bus takes a snow emergency route to Columbia Road, but it still gets me to school."

My dad smiles. Because he understands exactly what the snow emergency route has to do with Miri's gymnastics meet, or at least he trusts that I understand.

"Thanks so much, Gilah, for solving that schedule puzzle," my mom says. "The world needs more people who can find different ways of doing things."

I'm really grinning then, because with three kids, figuring out other people's schedule puzzles has always been a big part of my mom's life, and while I know she likes being a mom, I think that scheduling is probably not her favorite part.

"Anytime," I say. "Always glad to help find a detour!"

ONE MORE

The caterer asks my mom for the final number of kids who are coming, and she says, "Fourteen," which is the kids in my class minus Grace who is out of town plus my cousins and my brother and sister and me.

I'm on the other side of the family room, listening to music on headphones, which for me means that my brain is making pictures of how my body can be part of the music when I'm breakdancing, but my mom's answer breaks through and I call out to correct her.

"Actually fifteen."

My mom stops talking, and the catering guy smiles.

"Gilah?"

"What?"

"Did Grace say something at school?"

"No."

"Then I think we're at fourteen: the rest of your class and your cousin Caleb and—"

"I invited my new friend."

That got her quiet. I think she is better at telling people, "Gilah can do anything!" when the "anything" includes things that have been pre-approved by her in advance. Or maybe she just didn't expect me to make a new friend she didn't know about: before I took the bus, there were a lot fewer times in the day when she didn't know who I was talking to.

"What new friend?" she asks.

"His name is Guillermo. We ride the bus together."

My mom smiles then, but it isn't a "friend" smile or a "jerk who is not worth my time" smile. Back when Asher and I were studying those flash cards, I remember Miri pointing out, "There's lots more kinds of smiles than that. There's smiles like you make at a little kid when you don't believe what they're saying." Asher said not to confuse me, that the important thing was that I stop getting picked on by people who were smiling at me like jerks who are not worth my time. I agreed with Asher but wanted to hear more about what Miri meant about those other kinds of smiles.

It turns out there isn't a flash card deck that is big enough for every kind of smile.

Like maybe my mom is smiling now because she isn't sure whether to believe that I made a new friend she doesn't know about and successfully told him when and where my bat mitzvah is. Back when she had to drive me everywhere, it wouldn't have been physically possible for me to meet a new friend she didn't know about.

The catering guy smiles too. He probably sees lots of almost-thirteen-year-olds with their parents, so I smile to see him smile and imagine that the conversation that my mom and I are having is exactly like lots of other almost-bat-and-bar mitzvah kids, finally old enough to make their own friends.

"We'll have plenty of food," he assures both of us.

LESSON

At my bat mitzvah lesson, I do a final run-through of the blessings before and after the Haftarah. It's actually easier singing all this stuff in Hebrew when I don't know what most of it means. It's when people know what they're saying that their words and their meaning can contradict each other.

So the hardest part is my speech, which is in English. Not only will I know what the words mean, but I'm supposed to say what words to use and what order to use them in.

"Do I have to do a speech?" I've asked Josh approximately every other week since my lessons started last spring.

At first, he answered the same way every time, an answer that wasn't exactly "yes" or "no." "Well," he'd tell me, "Everyone has something to say: maybe you could think about what you have to say that's unique, that other people won't think of on their own."

But what can I say that other people won't think of on their own but is worth their time thinking about?

I have no idea. But I know someone who has a very unique way of figuring things out. He writes poems. And he's not like the people who wrote their poems hundreds of years ago and had to be dead for a long time before anyone would read them. He's a kid my age who writes poems. And his poems come in two different languages.

MICHAELA

The one thing we don't have in our home gym is rings from the ceiling. If we had rings, I'd probably be there all the time, and probably it would be a huge fight every time someone wanted to use the room for anything else, like Asher is doing with his friend Michaela right now. Whatever they are doing down there, they are not making noise on the equipment like Miri does with her friends when they hang out down there. And I do not hear sounds like someone punching a chess clock.

Miri's friends are different. For one thing, I don't know most of their names. If I thought it was important, I could pay close attention to which one has purple braces and which one has pierced ears and details like that, but it's frustrating when people do things like change the color of their braces or don't wear earrings sometimes despite having holes drilled in their head for that purpose.

It's not like I ever need to call any of them by name, because the only conversation I would make with any of them would either be:

(a) in an emergency, such as if showers of plaster were about to rain on their head, or

(b) small talk, such as about the weather or how

their summer is going. (This is a case where having a common interest in avoiding small talk does not give us something to talk about, despite what Ms. Perl told us in social learning class.)

In an emergency, it's hard to know whether the seconds used to shout someone's name would result in a shorter time to get their attention (and for them to react) as opposed to costing precious time that they could be using to move out of the way of falling plaster (for example).

So far, the only time I have had to speak out in an emergency was when Guillermo fell off his bike. And that did not yield data that are useful to this question because I did not see the emergency until after it happened, and also the bus windows were closed, so I would not have been able to call out to him (with or without his name). I could only call out to other people on the bus.

If it took twelve and a half years for me to face my first emergency, even if the next emergency comes in half the amount of time, it is unlikely that Miri's current friends will be involved, given that we will all be grown-ups by then. Likely enough, anyway, that it is not worth learning their names.

The name of Asher's friend Michaela stands out, because Michaela is a girl's name that is based off a boy's name (Michael), but this Michaela looks enough like a boy and enough like a girl that when I first met Michaela, when I was about eight, I asked, "Are you a boy or a girl?"

"Gilah!" said Asher, but Michaela just smiled and asked me (in a voice that was a little like a boy's voice and a little like a girl's voice), "What do you think?"

"I don't know," I answered, and Michaela never told me. Later, when I came across the term "nonbinary," that made a lot of sense. Because as much as I sometimes like categories, I really like knowing that people are bigger than categories and that categories don't always fit. Maybe that is something the rest of the world might like to know too.

PUSH-UPS

To show what a good job I do with sharing the gym/downstairs, I do push-ups in my room.

I started soon after we got my bat mitzvah date assigned, and I decided I wanted to be strong enough to do a backflip while breakdancing at the party. When I started, I could do eight push-ups in a row, and now I can almost always do twenty-three.

Being able to do a backflip requires at least two things:

(a) arm strength, and

(b) courage to let myself fly in the air.

And in this case (b) is directly influenced by (a)—a.k.a., I will be more likely to be brave if I am also strong. And being strong is within my control. But so far, being strong and brave has not added up to being able to do a backflip.

I can tell I'm getting closer, though, because my mom will say things like, "Gilah, is that safe?" and "Be careful, sweetie!" more than when she thought I was just playing around on the floor. Once or twice she even asked, "Is there some kind of coach or place that gives lessons in breakdancing?"

"Maybe!" I answered. Breakdancing isn't the kind of club that happens at school, like Asher got started in his chess club, or the kind of activity where everyone you know is taking lessons, like how Miri first signed up for gymnastics. Part of me thinks it would be great to have breakdancing be an activity the whole family took seriously, and where I could have a coach help me learn things more quickly. But part of me also likes having breakdancing be just for me sometimes, something I can do when and where I want to. If signing up would take breakdancing to a different level for me, is that a hundred percent a good thing?

I am surprised, but only a little bit, to come into my room one night and find three instructional diagrams on how to do a backflip, which have been slid under the door. They were left anonymously, which means whoever dropped them off did not want to be identified, but I can take a pretty good guess based on who has a key to our house and also knows how much I want to learn to backflip.

I have a blue rug in the middle of my floor, with checkered squares of dark blue and light blue—with a mat underneath that my mom insisted I put there for extra protection. I always make sure that my left hand is on a light blue square and my right hand on dark blue. Until recently, that meant my left foot was on dark blue and my right foot was on light blue, but then I hit a growth spurt this summer and I finally figured out that I was no longer at the right angle if I kept myself on those same squares.

"It's not fair," I tell Asher. "Why should I waste time figuring out something I already figured out before?"

"For chess I use pictures," Asher points out.

I smile, but he does not mention the backflip pictures under my door.

"But you don't have to do that in chess," I say. "Once you know something, you know it."

"Only sort of," Asher says. "I can know something that works on some opponents, but as my rating improves the opponents get harder. So the new opponents know how to defend against whatever attack I spent all those weeks learning, so I have to learn all over again how to think like them."

I try to imagine that. Figuring out how other people think isn't easy—maybe for anyone—even if whatever I learn will probably sort of kind of apply to the next person too. Although a rating system, like they have in chess, would be helpful. People rated between X and X + 100, I should do Y. For ratings between X + 101 and X + 300, I should do Z.

"Anyway," Asher says, "Pictures help. I put them above my bed and kind of look at them when I'm semi-conscious, to help them stick."

Usually I like my walls white, as a break from all the noise my brain is busy sorting out. Asher knows that. But he also knows how talking about all those different kinds of smiles, with or without the flash cards, helped me a lot too.

"You don't have to leave them up forever," he says. "Miri has some kind of putty she uses to hang stuff up at camp."

"And she let you have some?"

"Yeah." Asher shrugs. "Just ask her when she's in a good mood."

I hesitate. "I don't think she's ever in a good mood around me. It's like my existence puts her in a bad mood or something."

"Don't let her bother you," Asher says. "She's one of those people who just floats through life in a cloud of drama. Wherever she goes, the drama just kind of surrounds her."

That image makes me smile, especially when I imagine Miri giving orders that her drama cloud isn't puffy enough or doesn't have the right kind of sparkle.

"I've learned to use it to my advantage," Asher says.

That piques my interest. "Really?"

"If there's one person in a family who wants the whole world to pay attention to her, it means other people can kind of do what they want sometimes without anyone noticing. Sometimes that can be really useful."

"So you don't think she hates me personally?"

"Oh, I know she doesn't," Asher says. "She actually told me once—well, I'm probably not supposed to say anything."

I watch Asher struggle with two rules that are telling him to do opposite things: the rule about not telling other people a secret someone asked you to keep, and the rule about not withholding information that can fix someone's problem. I can be as patient as I need to be, that's how glad I am not to be the only one struggling with opposing rules.

"OK," Asher decides. "Miri told me once that she wishes she could be more like you." My eyebrows go up.

"Yeah," Asher says. "She said most people have so much noise around us, people thinking we should be one thing or another, it can be really hard to figure out who you are. But you always find a way to be yourself."

I'm still surprised as I let that sink in: if Miri (and maybe Asher too) thinks I don't have noise from people telling me I should be more one way or another, they clearly haven't been paying much attention to all the people telling me to be more socially appropriate. But the idea that Miri, and maybe Asher too, and maybe everyone else has some kind of noise in their heads too—and the fact that Miri wants to be more like me— that is all very good news.

PUTTY

Thursday nights Miri is sometimes in a good mood if her gymnastics class went well. I find her in the basement doing one-handed cartwheels and sit and wait for her to finish.

"Hi," I say when she stops cartwheeling and looks my way.

"What," she says, flat, in one tone, which means "What do you want?" The other kind of "What?"—which goes up at the end—means, "I didn't hear you." I've started to notice that Miri uses pretty much the annoyed-sounding "What?" with everyone, not just me, so I don't take it personally.

"Asher said you have putty," I say, which doesn't come out the way I practiced it, when it makes perfect sense even to people who don't live in my head.

"Wha-at?" says Miri, two syllables this time. This means, "What are you talking about?" which is actually an improvement over "What."

"Putty, to hang stuff up with," I explain. "He said you use it at sleepover camp, so it doesn't leave a mark on the wall."

"Do I have a sign on my head that says CVS?" she asks, which is a non sequitur and also a rhetorical question at the same time, which means I'm not expected to answer.

Miri sighs.

"You'd think as the youngest person in the family I wouldn't be the only one who had mastered how to buy office supplies. But I'll give you some putty as long as you don't want glow-in-the-dark. How much do you need?"

I had never heard of glow-in-the-dark putty, so it's a relief that I won't accidentally end up with some. But I also don't know what kind of units putty comes in to know how much to answer.

It occurs to me that I could stop in an actual CVS—there is one very close to both of my bus stops—and do some research on putty. Then Miri wouldn't have to feel like people expect her to be older than she is, like she is the keeper of office supplies. I know how it feels when people treat you like a different age than you are.

Going to CVS is a great idea, but it won't get me putty tonight. And it wouldn't be free: I'd have to pay for more than I actually need.

Miri sighs. "Why don't you come back when you know how much you need?"

"Three pictures!" I blurt out. "I need however much putty would hang up three pictures."

"Fine," she says. "When I come up later."

I go upstairs, and eventually, later, I hear Miri come upstairs.

But then she takes a shower and does whatever else she does, so I think maybe she forgot. I leave my room just long enough to brush my teeth, and when I come back, there's a small tin of putty in the middle of my bed, where I won't miss it.

It turns out to be more than I need for three pictures, which I hang on my closet door.

THE CONTEST

On Tuesday morning when Guillermo gets on the bus, he sits across the aisle from me, but after we say hello, he is mostly writing-writing-writing, and I don't think he even notices what kind of smile I give him when we say hello.

He just sits at the front of the bus, writing-writing-writing something, like I wasn't even here.

He's so busy writing-writing-writing that he doesn't look up when the bus stops near his school.

A rule of riding the bus is that you should try not to block the aisle and delay people from getting on. This is being a good passenger. However, if someone you know seems like they might be about to miss their stop, it is also nice not to keep your mouth shut. This is being a good friend. So I decide that being a good friend outranks being a good passenger, and the people who just got on can just wait for another three seconds to find their seats.

I stand up and say, "Hi, Guillermo, we're at your stop." I have to talk loudly because of the bus engine and the man across the aisle on his phone and the toddler playing a noisy video game.

Guillermo's head jerks up from what he was writing, looking surprised like he had just been asleep, and he quickly gathers his notebook and things into his backpack.

Of course, my original seat is no longer available, so I stay where I am while Guillermo gets out of his seat, which I know is about to become empty.

He still looks dazed, like he just woke up. But he looks back at me and smiles a smile that has never appeared on any flash card or any other face, but somehow I know what it means.

"Hey, thanks, Gilah," he says.

"No problem," I say.

I think I forget to smile back.

The next morning I'm not thinking totally clearly, because my toothpaste was empty that morning and I had to share Asher's, even though he wasn't even home to ask, because his is the only other kind of toothpaste that doesn't make me gag. So I'm not gagging but I'm also not focused on anything other than the fact that my mouth does not taste right, so the bus is almost at Guillermo's stop before I can even think about smiling. When I finally smile, I think it ends up as a combination of the two smiles.

Guillermo smiles when he gets on, sort of the same smile as the day before, and then I forget to worry about smiling because we are having a conversation. What happens is that he pulls a folded square of pink paper out of his pocket and starts turning it around in his hands without opening it or looking at it.

There is a rule that you should not ask people what is in their pockets, but there is also a rule that sometimes if someone wants you to notice something such as a new pair of glasses or a new necklace, they will touch it a lot without saying anything because they want you to comment on it first.

I am trying to remember if that rule ever applies to a piece of paper, and I decide that it can, because what if it is an award or a really amazing report card or something? Even though Asher gets a lot of both of those, and I can't remember him ever folding one of those up and fidgeting with it until someone comments, and also those types of documents do not usually come on pink paper.

However, the paper is no longer in Guillermo's pocket, so the rule about no-pocket-asking no longer applies, and I don't want to hurt his feelings by not asking about it if he wants me to.

So I say, "What's on the paper?"

He looks at it like he is surprised, like he doesn't know how it got out of his pocket, which makes me think I shouldn't have asked. On the other hand, he is probably aware of the rule about if you don't want people to be interested in it, the safest place for it is at home, which applies mostly to toys that you don't want the rest of the class playing with but could also apply to folded pink paper if the paper is not something you want to answer questions about.

He opens it and hands it to me:

POETRY CONTEST

How to enter: All students may enter one poem in the style of your choosing. Poem must be your own original work. Please submit your typed or neatly printed poem to Ms. Díaz in room 174, by November 13th.

Prize: $100 for the winning poet, and the opportunity to recite your poem at Busboys and Poets!

Winner will be selected by the English Department and announced on the November 16th morning announcements.

I say, "That's perfect for you!" I see how hard he is writing-writing-writing while he rides the bus, and I know suddenly that he is writing more poems like the one he gave me to RSVP to my bat mitzvah, only he must have ideas of other things to write about because he already gave me that answer and nobody gets invited to a bat mitzvah every single day.

So he has lots of ideas plus a willingness to work hard, which I figure is most of what he needs to win a poetry contest (plus maybe some good luck, which is not in anyone's control). But when he doesn't bounce up and down and say *of course* he'll enter, I remember one more thing he needs: courage to take a chance.

"Hey," I say. "There's prize money. If you win, you can pay for your bike repairs."

Guillermo's smile starts in his eyes. From there it radiates to his forehead and down to his cheeks, where there is a little dimple the perfect size for storing ideas for poems. It spreads wider until his ears (or at least the ear next to me, I have to imagine the other one) turns pink and then finally his mouth turns upward and his teeth peek through—

And I officially stop analyzing his smile long enough to smile with him.

SNEAKY

On Thursday I break the rule about scooting all the way over to the window seat so someone else can sit on the aisle. I sit in the aisle seat myself and wait to see if anyone will point out that I'm breaking a rule, but nobody does.

Also, nobody sits in the empty window seat, since that would mean climbing over me. I think people are not happy about climbing in general, since that means touching someone who is not in your family and not your friend and who might be sweaty or sticky even if you can't tell by looking at them.

Sitting in the aisle seat is sneaky because now when Guillermo gets on, I move directly to the window seat and he sits next to me.

I smile but do not consult a diagram.

SITTING

When Guillermo and I talk to each other, neither of us minds if what the other person says is a non sequitur.

For example, I don't think it's technically a non sequitur when I notice a man on a bench who is playing a guitar, and on the ground in front of him is a plastic bucket with some dollar bills in it, and I tell Guillermo, "It's too bad you don't play an instrument. You could get a lot of money for your bike. You know, in case, the contest doesn't work out."

Some people's feelings might be hurt because I didn't automatically assume he'd win the contest.

Guillermo doesn't say anything. But I think maybe his feelings aren't hurt.

Because we know each other well enough now that sometimes, we can ride together quietly without talking.

And sometimes, riding together quietly can be a way to learn something amazing.

HOW GUILLERMO WRITES A POEM

Guillermo writes down some words in his notebook.

He crosses out some of the words and keeps other ones not crossed out.

He adds more words.

He takes out more words.

He draws an arrow so he can put some of the words in between other words.

He turns the paper sideways to fit in different words.

Then he crosses some of them out.

Guillermo writing a poem is kind of like making up a dance.

HOW I FINALLY WRITE MY
BAT MITZVAH SPEECH

I write down some words on the computer downstairs.

I delete some of the words and keep other ones not deleted.

I add more words.

I take out more words.

I turn the laptop sideways in case that changes how I want to say things.

I type some of the words in between other words.

Then I delete some of them.

Writing a bat mitzvah speech is like Guillermo writing a poem. And both of them are like making up a dance.

GUILLERMO

SILVER LININGS

I'm still not happy my bike is broken,
but like my mom says,
"No hay mal que por bien no venga."
Which means
there is no bad, from which good does not come,
which sounds kind of confusing in English,
so maybe it's better to give a similar saying
which is: Every cloud has a silver lining.
And the silver lining of my bike being broken,
is riding the H4
and talking with Gilah.

THE PINK PAPER

When I put my cold hands
into the pocket of my coat
(which is my father's coat,
since I still haven't found mine)
my fingers find a folded note,
a square of paper
I had forgotten about.

Gilah asks to see it.
Unfolded
in her hands,
are words printed
on pink paper—the poetry contest.

She tells me
I should enter
but she has only seen
one
very small
poem of mine.

Gilah is the only non-teacher

who knows I write poetry,

except for my cousin Mayra,

who promised not to tell our other cousins,

because they would call me "Shakespeare" or something,

just to mess with me,

or they would say some immature thing,

like,

Roses are red,

violets are blue,

Guillermo writes poems,

that smell like Alex's shoe.

"Hey," Gilah says,

and points to the bottom of

the pink paper.

"There's prize money.

If you win, you can pay for your bike repairs."

The prize is one hundred dollars.

More than enough to fix my bike,

and even some extra to help my parents.

But at home,

when I pull the pink paper out again,

I notice something else.

Along with the prize money,

the winner will recite their poem

at a place called Busboys and Poets.

The idea of reciting my poetry

in front of people

makes my arms look like

chicken skin

before it's dropped

into boiling water.

BUS ROUTES

PART I

I'm not supposed to leave
the boundaries of
Columbia Heights
and Park View
without asking permission
unless I'm going to school,
but I do.

Ms. Díaz says,
"Write what you know,"
so I'm trying to know more,
so I can write more.

If I'm back by
twilight, I'm sure
my parents won't notice
my absence
as I have a habit

of disappearing
and they have a habit
of being preoccupied
with things other than me,
at least since we moved here.

So, I leave Northwest altogether,
riding buses I've never ridden before
to see as much of DC as I can.

PART II

Bus routes
are like the blood vessels of a city;
blue veins and red arteries
bringing life
to a beating heart.

PART III

We pass Dupont Circle
where a man in a flat cap

and a teenage boy
play chess in the park.

We pass streets
that look like magical golden tunnels
because of the ginkgo trees
raining yellow leaves.

We pass a community garden
with a rusted red wheelbarrow
and a woman with a bandana
over her braided hair.
It's time to harvest
broccoli, Brussels sprouts,
spinach, cauliflower,
and kale
before the first blanket of snow
tucks the garden beds
in for the winter.

We pass a man playing drums
on overturned plastic buckets,

that sound like *thwack-thwack-thwack!*
and another
playing a slow song
on trumpet,
which makes you feel kind of sad.

We pass the Potomac River
which looks like a wide, dark ribbon
weaving between highways and trees.

We pass food trucks selling
Mexican tortas, Vietnamese pho, and Middle Eastern kabobs,
and nearby,
a man sitting on a bench,
eating chicken covered in
orange-red mumbo sauce
out of a brown clamshell container.

We pass Metro stops,
and coffee shops,
with people reading
in sunlit windows.

We pass monuments,

white like bone,

a woman who leads protesters,

and chants through a megaphone.

We pass by many things

out on the streets,

but I wonder when DC

will feel like home

to me.

PART IV

Back on the H4
when I see Gilah's empty seat,
I finally know what
my poem will be.

I write it in my notebook,
then make one copy
for Ms. Díaz,
and another
as a gift for Gilah.

CONSEQUENCES

PART I

I was wrong
about my parents
not noticing
my absence.

They are both waiting for me
at the kitchen table
when I come in.

My punishment is
three days without my bike.

My mom holds out her hand
for the key to my bike lock,
but the key is on my dresser
in my bedroom
instead of in my pocket

because I don't have a bike
to lock up at the moment.

PART II

"Guillermo, ¿Dónde está tu bicicleta?"
I hang my head.

There is a difference between
lying by omission,
(which is lying by not saying something)
and regular lying.
Although my mother would say
they're both equally wrong,
regular lying is harder.
But even harder than regular lying,
is telling the truth.

PART III

I tell my parents
the whole story

about the crash.
Even the part
about me falling down.
I tell them too,
that I rode buses
other than the H4
to places beyond
our neighborhood
and school.
I get a lecture
on
responsibilidad,
honestidad,
and
seguridad.

Since they can't take my bike away,
my punishment for lying is that I need to
earn the money to fix it myself.

When I say,

"I was already doing that anyway,"

My father asks me, "¿Y qué querés vos? Otro castigo?"

I shake my head no.

I would not like another punishment.

AND THE WINNER IS...

PART I

When the overhead speaker
in my first period class
crackles to life,
my heartbeat takes off
like a racehorse
galloping, galloping, galloping.

Today is the day the winner of the poetry contest will be
announced.

I shake my legs
side to side
listening
and waiting
as
Vice Principal Nguyen announces
the date
and

the Pledge of Allegiance

and

the weather

and

the lunch menu

and

a reminder to turn in permission slips for a field trip

and

that the robotics club will not be meeting today

and

finally

she passes the microphone to Ms. Díaz

for a "special announcement."

Ms. Díaz clears her throat

and says,

"All of the students who entered the poetry contest

should be very proud.

All of the entries were very good,

but after careful consideration

the English department unanimously agreed,

and the winner is…"

And then she says a name
that is not mine.

PART II

The first poem I ever wrote was an accident,
which makes me wonder if I'm even a poet.
It happened the summer Araceli was born,
they came into the world at the same time,
except my sister was born in Maryland,
and my poem was born in West Virginia.

The first poem I ever wrote was an accident.
My parents left me at Grandma Maureen and Grandpa Jack's
house,
to prepare for Araceli's arrival,
especially since my mom was having complications,
and the doctor said she needed to rest.
I didn't understand why they sent me to Grandma and
Grandpa's house,
it would have made more sense for my mother to go,
since it was nothing but quiet there.

The first poem I ever wrote was an accident.

There were no cousins running around to play with.

It was just the three of us, and their dog Rags, who didn't like children.

On the wall along the staircase were photos of my mother growing up,

a photo of my parents' wedding,

a few photos of me.

Soon there would be one of my baby sister.

But until then, I was alone.

The first poem I ever wrote was an accident.

We played board games in the evenings,

mostly Scrabble, Grandma's favorite.

Except she knew more words than me, so she always won—

a fact I pointed out to her after losing yet again.

The first poem I ever wrote was an accident.

Grandma gave me a journal and a pen,

told me to write down any words I hear and don't know,

so we can look them up in the dictionary together every night

at bedtime.

"You'll be a master Scrabble player in no time," she smiled.
So I wrote down the words.

The first poem I ever wrote was an accident.
The first day, my list of words looked like this:

subterranean

metropolis

night crawler

sanctuary

When Grandma read my list that night she said,
"It looks like you've written a poem."
After I knew the meaning of the words,
I could see what she meant.

The first poem I ever wrote was an accident.
The words made a picture in my mind
of the thick worms Grandpa called night crawlers
safe underneath the cold, dark dirt,
a whole city of them.

I started trying to put my new words together
to make poems on purpose.
It kept me busy that summer at my grandparents' house,
but I didn't stop, even when I went home.
I liked creating pictures with words.

Since we moved, writing poems hasn't been so much for
creating pictures.
I didn't realize it until now, but poetry helps me figure out
how I feel.
Since we moved, writing poems has been a way of talking to
myself,
of saying the things I would have trusted to Mayra if she were
here.

But the first poem I ever wrote was an accident,
which makes me wonder if I'm even a poet.

PART III

Maybe I'm not a poet.
Maybe I shouldn't write
any more poems.

That is all I can think about
all day long.

But then I remember
how I feel when I write,
like my pen and paper
make anything possible.
I remember that
I didn't start writing poems
to win contests.

I started writing poems because
words can
paint pictures
like watercolor windows
opened

letting in light
opened
letting out what weighs
me down.

PART IV

I'm OK about not winning
the poetry contest
but now I need a new plan
to raise money
to pay for my bike,
and I am out of plans
at the moment.

ENGLISH CLASS

PART I

English/Language Arts with Ms. Díaz
is my last class of the day
so when there's only a few minutes to go
my feet feel like
two dogs ready to run
and my legs are leashes
holding them back.

PART II

Ms. Díaz says we can pack up
and the classroom fills with the sounds of
books slamming closed,
chairs screeching,
and backpacks zipping
but
Ms. Díaz
raises her voice

above the noise
to say,
"Guillermo,"
as she tucks her dark, bobbed hair
behind her ears,
and then shuffles some papers.
When she looks up
and waves me over,
I wonder
what am I in trouble for now.

PART III

"Guillermo,"
Ms. Díaz says again
when I arrive at her desk.
"I really loved your poem
about your friend Gilah."

It feels weird to hear someone
who doesn't know Gilah,
say her name,

and I can tell from Ms. Díaz's expression
that she thinks Gilah is a girlfriend
instead of a girl ----- friend
which makes my ears burn hot,
and probably makes Ms. Díaz
think that she's right,
when the truth is
maybe Ms. Díaz
has been watching too many
telenovelas.

"Gracias," I answer in Spanish.
"Ella es una buena amiga."
She is a good friend, I say.
Because in Spanish
amiga = female friend
and
novia = girlfriend.
I like that in Spanish,
the words sound
very different.

That way,

there can be no misunderstandings.

PART IV

"There has been a misunderstanding,"

Ms. Díaz tells me.

"Busboys and Poets

has invited all students,

not just the winner,

to recite their poems,

so I wanted to make sure you knew.

I would love to see you

and your family there."

She hands me a flyer

with the date, time, and location.

I start to explain

that Araceli has been sick lately,

so my parents probably can't make it,

and Sunday is a "family day"

so I probably can't come on my own,

but the bell rings
and Ms. Díaz just says,
"Think about it."

PART V

When I think about
stepping up on a stage
in front of a crowd
to speak my words
into a microphone
something inside me
feels like when
Mayra convinced me
to ride the Wave Swinger ride
at the Montgomery County Fair.

It felt like flying,
but also like
the chains might
snap

and send me, and my seat
flying for real
three hundred feet
above the fairgrounds
and into the parking lot.
But after a minute
of feeling like that
I started to trust
the cold metal chains
in my hands
and the wind
in my hair
and there was disappointment
in my heart
when the ride slowed
then
came to a stop.

Maybe
reading my poems aloud
might feel like that.

STILL SICK

On delivery days
my dad appreciates my help at the bakery
even more
because I can carry sacks of flour
from the truck
that weigh fifty pounds each
which is easy
because I just pretend it's Araceli.

Araceli weighs forty-nine pounds
and I pick her up all the time
on and off swings at the park
when she wants to make a sandwich
"by herself"
but needs help reaching the peanut butter,
and when my mom takes forever at the bookstore
and Araceli sinks down to the floor
like our neighbors' cat Miss Mochi,
and refuses to walk.

But lately I don't pick her up
because Araceli isn't feeling well,
and she stays on the sofa
sleeping
still
as a little
sack of flour.

(3 x 4) x B = 300

I can only stay
a few minutes more.
If I stay any longer
I'll miss the H4 to school.
But the bakery has a big order,
and my father needs me.

The Embassy of El Salvador
is hosting an event
and Mr. Sandoval ordered so many cookies
that the white boxes stacked on the front counter
are taller than my father,
who is counting, checking,
and double-checking
to make sure
nothing is missing.

Each box contains
4 semitas, 4 quesadillas, and 4 marquesotes.
There are 25 boxes

because Mr. Sandoval

said he wanted 300 pastries.

I never realized how much math I do,

outside of Mr. Whitaker's classroom.

But when my dad asked me to figure out

how many boxes we'd need,

I used this equation:

$(3 \times 4) \times b = 300$

There are 3 types of pastries,

4 of each per box,

because a box fits one dozen.

You do parentheses first

so $12 \times b = 300$.

12 pastries per box,

300 pastries total,

but how many boxes?

So I thought hard

and imagined Mr. Whitaker up at the board,

and somehow I knew,

I needed to divide 300 by 12

to solve for the variable.

So b = 25.

When my dad sees my equation
scratched onto a scrap of receipt paper
he smiles and nods.

$10

Mr. Sandoval is an elegant man
as my abuela Mamá Tomasa would say
"un hombre elegante."

He wears wire frame glasses,
a slim-fitting suit,
and a smile that shines as bright
as his polished black shoes.

I stack the last of the boxes
into the trunk of his car
just as the H4 comes into view
down the street.

"¡Que tenga un buen día, señor!"
I say, so I can rush away,
but Mr. Sandoval
catches my shoulder, thanks me,
and presses a folded bill into my palm.

When he gets into his car,
I take a peek,
and can't believe
what I see.

$10 is almost enough to get my bicycle back,
with my $6.61, I'm now only $3.39 short,
But my parents could use this money too.

I hold the ten dollars out to my dad
but he shakes his head.
"That's your tip, Guillermo. You earned it.
Now hurry before you're late for school."

BUSKING

PART I

On the bus,
I tell Gilah
about losing the poetry contest,
and Mr. Sandoval's tip,
and how close
yet how far
I am
to getting my bicycle back.
She thinks for a moment,
looks out the window
with the pink eraser of her pencil
tapping her lips
then gives me the best idea
I never thought of.

PART II

After school I get off the bus early
at the spot where Gilah
pointed out the guitar-playing man
on the bench
this morning.

He is still here,
white beard like Santa Claus,
in an Army green coat,
and a hoodie pulled up
over a red knit cap.

He isn't busking right now.
Right now, he sits with his hands,
the same rich brown color of his mahogany guitar,
folded over his stomach,
his legs outstretched,
eyes closed.

I sit down,

pen and paper at the ready,

but how are people to know

what I'm selling,

or that I'm selling anything at all?

When one plays guitar,

he need only play,

and set out a case or a hat

to collect coins,

but when one writes poems,

it is not obvious

what exactly they're doing.

PART III

I ask a woman with curly hair

if she'd like to buy a poem,

but she has earbuds in her ears

and without looking at me,

she keeps walking.

I ask a man walking a dog
if he'd like to buy a poem,
but he wraps the leash
tighter around his wrist
and keeps walking.

I ask an older woman jogging,
two women carrying groceries,
a couple holding hands,
a man waiting at the bus stop.

An hour passes,
and I haven't sold
even one poem.

A flock of pigeons
flap their grey wings
and land by my feet
strutting and cooing
picking at crumbs
near the trash can.

"I guess none of you
want to buy a poem either?"
I mumble, and
the man next to me,
the man with a beard like Santa Claus,
the man who I thought was sleeping,
laughs.

PART IV

His name is Henry.
(I call him Mr. Henry, because it's more respectful.)
It turns out
he likes poetry too.
He reaches into a shopping cart
which is filled with
flattened cardboard boxes,
blankets,
and bulging black trash bags,
and he pulls out a
black and white composition book.

The worn pages flip under his thumb,
and they are all filled
to the margins
with cursive blue ink
which he says are lyrics
to some of the songs
he plays on his guitar.

PART V

Not all buskers are homeless,
and not all people who are homeless are buskers,
but Mr. Henry is both.
When I ask him how he became
homeless,
he says, "That's a long story,"
and plays a song on his guitar
for me instead
about a man
whose heart was so broken
all he could do
was cry all day,

until his tears made a river,
to wash his troubles away.

I can't tell if the song is
autobiographical,
'cause Mr. Henry smiles
when he sings it.

PART VI

"Why don't you try performing your poetry?"
Mr. Henry says, as he tugs on his beard.
"Might make more money like that."

"Like, just start reading it aloud?" I say.
"Right here on this bench?"

Mr. Henry nods.

"Don't you think people might laugh?
Or think my poems aren't any good?" I say.
"I've found it never

does any good to worry what other folks might think of me."
Mr. Henry shrugs.

PART VII

I think about the poems
on notebook paper
in the darkness of my backpack,
and try to imagine the words
flying off the page
out into the golden sunlight,
landing like leaves
on the sidewalk
in the street
for everyone,
not just me.

PART VIII

When I think about reading
my poetry aloud,
why does my mouth go dry

like I've eaten a mouthful of pan dulce
with nothing to wash it down?

PART IX

I tell Mr. Henry about the invitation
to recite my poetry
at Busboys and Poets,
but admit
I probably won't go
because my sister is sick,
and my parents say Sunday is "family day"
which means we don't go anywhere on our own,
and also, it's a day after my friend's bat mitzvah,
so I'll be too tired anyway.

Mr. Henry looks at me, without turning his head,
his lips pressed together, and says,
"That sounds like a whole lot of excuses."

When I ask what he means,

he says,
"Sometimes it's easier
to pretend something
is holding you back
when that something
is really yourself."

And I realize
Mr. Henry knows
what I haven't told him.
Mr. Henry knows
that part of me is really
just not brave enough
to recite my poetry.

Not up on stage
at Busboys and Poets.
Not even here
on this park bench.

LANGSTON HUGHES

PART I

"Do you know
how the place
Busboys and Poets
got its name?"
Mr. Henry asks.

I shake my head,
and he shakes his head too,
but when he shakes his head
it's in a "that's a shame" sort of way.

"Youngblood," he says,
"let me tell you a story,
about a busboy poet
named Langston Hughes.

Langston worked,
cleaning dishes off tables,

at a restaurant here in DC

inside the Wardman Park Hotel.

While working one day

Langston noticed

a famous poet sitting at one of the tables,

so he took out three sheets of paper,

wrote down three of his poems,

and slipped them

under the man's plate.

Soon the whole world knew

of the busboy poet

Langston Hughes,

but it wouldn't have happened

if he hadn't been bold,

if he cleared the dishes—silent

not telling a soul.

It wouldn't have happened,

if he hadn't seized the opportunity in his hands,

to show that man,

who he was,

who he really was,

not just a busboy,

but a poet too."

PART II

When I ask Mr. Henry to tell me more

about Langston Hughes,

he reaches a hand into a bag in his cart,

and when it surfaces,

it's holding a worn yellow book.

The book is a short biography,

and includes some of Langston's poetry.

The more I read,

the more I realize,

Langston and I have a lot in common.

Not only are we both poets,

we both had to move,

and change schools.

Langston learned to speak many languages,
including English and Spanish—like me,
and although he wasn't born here,
at one time he lived in DC.

But one thing Langston had,
that I do not
is bravery.

PART III

(Inspired by the style of Mr. Langston Hughes)

O, that I could grow it
like a fragrant garden flower
O, that it would come to me
like the bedtime hour.

O, that I could put it on
like a velvet sash
O, that I could work for it
or pay for it with cash.

O, that I could bake it
like one of Papá's pies
or win it in a contest
as a shining prize.

O, but the conclusion
at which I have arrived
is that bravery
is only found inside.

PART IV

When I tell Mr. Henry
I should get going,
and that the H4 will be
coming any minute,
instead of saying goodbye
he starts strumming his guitar
and singing a song
that goes:
You must take the H4
to go to Wisconsin Avenue

way up in Tenleytown.

If you miss the H4

you'll find you missed

the quickest way to get

to Tenleytown.

Hurry, get on, now it's coming.

Listen to those brakes a-screeching.

All aboard, get on the H4.

Soon you will be on Wisconsin Avenue

in Tenleytown.

PART V

I don't make any money

busking poetry,

but some things

are more valuable than money

anyway.

ON THE HOUSE

Bruno's Bicycles & Repair
is filled with more than bicycles today,
people fill the store,
but beyond them at the counter,
Ryan waves hello.
When he finishes with a customer,
he motions me to the garage
so I step behind the counter
(and over Bruno, who is chewing on a tennis ball).

My bicycle looks better than brand new,
it's been polished to a shine.
Not only do the wheels not wobble,
they are fresh and perfectly aligned.
I'm also surprised to find
it no longer squeaks and squeals,
my bicycle is smooth and silent,
when I turn the handlebars
and when I move the wheels.

"I found some good spare parts,
and gave you a tune-up," Ryan says.
I hold out the cash,
sixteen dollars and sixty-one cents,
explain that it isn't enough
and start to ask if I can pay him
the rest later
but Ryan shakes his head.

"Business has picked up," he says,
and he doesn't think it's a coincidence
he's hearing more Spanish in his shop.
It's my ad bringing in customers,
and to show his thanks,
Ryan pats my back and says,
"This one's on the house."

THE HOSPITAL

PART I

The house is silent when I
close the door behind me.
My sister is
not bundled in blankets
on the sofa
watching *Angelina Ballerina*
(for the millionth time).

The sofa is empty.
The TV screen is black.

In the kitchen,
instead of my mother,
I find a cold cup of coffee,
and a note in rushed handwriting
with dotted *i*'s that look like comets
that makes my heart
drop.

PART II

The note tells me three things:

#1. My parents took Araceli to the hospital.

#2. Tía Carolina is on her way to watch me.

#3. I'm supposed to stay home and lock the door until she arrives.

PART III

The air is starting to chill
and a raindrop splashes
on the tip of my nose.
I pull my coat tight
and make sure
all the buttons
are fastened
before
riding into the night.

PART IV

I follow the same route
as the H4 takes
toward the hospital
but on my bicycle
at night
instead of in the warm seat
next to Gilah
the blur of headlights
and rush of traffic
so close
makes my heart beat
hard and fast
and the dark sky
feels like
it's closing around me
but I press my lips together
and keep pushing my feet
against the pedals.

PART V

The hospital doors whoosh
behind me
leaving the dark, wet night
outside,
except for the wetness
that followed me inside,
dripping from my hair
and untied shoelaces,
making my shoes squeak
on the bright, white
floor.

PART VI

The nurse shows me to a room
where my parents sit
vigilant
watching over Araceli
who is tucked into a bed
sleeping

with a plastic tube

plugging her tiny nose.

Her eyelids flutter open

like pale moth wings

when my shoes squeak

and she tries to sit up.

Her lips form the two identical syllables

of her apodo for me

but her voice

is a whisper.

PART VII

The nurse tells my father

in a voice that sounds like apology

that only parents can stay overnight

and that underage siblings

cannot.

My father leads me back down the hallway

to the elevator and presses the button.

His eyebrows are pushed together

like bookends
and the wrinkle between them
as thick as a dictionary.

He says something about
pneumonia, and her lungs
but when I try to ask
more questions,
he tells me
to go home.

I DON'T GO HOME

Two wheels
Steel frame
something real
something same
something mine
and mine alone
I ride my bike
I don't go home
even in
the slick quick rain
wet tennis shoes
clicking chain
my breath like ghosts
they float away
my tires slice
through puddles gray
And when I'm soaked
down to the bone
I turn around
and head back home.

GILAH

MISSING

My bat mitzvah tutor, Josh, has a Tree of Life picture on the wall behind his desk. It's a hologram, so it looks different when you see it from different angles. My chair that I sit on in there has wheels, which is how I've seen the Tree of Life picture from so many different angles. But I've never seen it from the angle of a dark office, behind a locked door.

My heart beats faster as I jiggle the smooth, metal handle. Four-fifteen on Wednesday, I'm positive, even though my phone is out of battery again. Where's Josh? The only way he wouldn't be here is if something terrible happened to him. He's not one of those people who comes late or forgets or is otherwise unreliable.

What could have happened? I pull harder on the handle, and the glass panel rattles but the light does not turn on and Josh does not appear.

Having a bat mitzvah means I'm a grown-up. What would a grown-up do if someone was missing, maybe needing help? What would my mom do if I was missing, if the door to my room was locked and the lights were off and I was not in the right place where I was supposed to be?

Of course, she would look for me.

VOLCANO

When Josh isn't where he's supposed to be, I race down to the lobby of the synagogue to tell my mom he needs our help. But my mom isn't texting or reading or trying to find two seconds to finish up a work project. She isn't there at all.

First Josh, then my mom. Panic rises like a wave of hot lava from the bottom of my stomach, swirling until it fills my mouth and my whole head.

It's like the volcano that we visited in Costa Rica, only it was so foggy that we never even saw the actual volcano that was supposedly right next to our hotel. It scared me so much that my mom and I flew home early, but even then I was terrified until my dad and Asher and Miri flew home as planned, three days later. If a whole volcano can go missing in the fog, despite staying planted exactly where it's been since the beginning of time, what are the chances of ever finding someone small like a person again if they aren't where they're supposed to be?

I race past the security guard who stands by the door of the synagogue and makes sure no one brings anything unsafe into the building. He doesn't look familiar, like maybe until today he was busy keeping some other place safe. Or maybe he has never kept anyplace else safe in his entire life, which scares me enough to make me run faster.

"Hey there, take it easy," he says, which is a comment that has no answer.

I run down the stairs outside the building where Miri and I used to climb on the handrail together before she discovered gymnastics and I discovered breakdancing. I sprint up to Connecticut Avenue and stand there panting, realizing that my mom and Josh could be literally anywhere, two different anywheres, maybe opposite directions from each other, and I have no idea how to find either of them.

I want to curl up and hide, but I'm on the street corner and there are puddles everywhere—there's nowhere to go—it's like I'm trapped on this wide-open space where any second, danger could come at me from any direction.

But then—at the top of the hill, I see what's coming toward me.

EAST

When the H4 comes down Porter Street at the exact minute I'm wishing for someplace to sit down with my knees pulled up and press my forehead against someplace cool while a soothing motion carries me along—it feels kind of like a salvation. I tap my DC One card and slide, with relief, into an empty two-seater.

With my eyes closed, breathing as deeply as I can, I wonder if this is how Joseph felt down there at the bottom of that pit. I imagine Joseph laying himself down on the cool earth at the bottom, covering himself with the coat of many colors, helping himself to feel calm.

When the bus gets to my school, of course school is closed, so there's no reason to get off. Mom and Josh are missing, which is another way to say the whole world is in chaos, and my therapists said that when everything feels chaotic, I need to cling to whatever bit of calmness I can find.

So I watch my school fade past and keep on being lulled by the cool window and the peaceful motion of the H4.

BROOKLAND

When I stop to think too hard about being on a part of the H4 bus route that I've never seen before, my heart beats faster and my throat makes little sounds that threaten to turn into a scream. But then I remember—my routine is already in chaos, Josh and my mom are both missing, and without them I might not have dinner tonight let alone a bat mitzvah on Saturday. The H4 is the one safe place I can look for them, resting my forehead against the cool plexiglass. Outside the world is chaos but the H4 goes back and forth, back and forth across the city. Outside are neighborhoods I've never seen before—how did I not know how big DC is, after living here my whole life?—

but inside the bus is familiar vinyl seats, familiar *dong!* when someone pulls the Stop Requested cord, familiar rocking like you don't get inside a car.

I wonder if I should have gotten off at my school. It's scary thinking about getting off the bus someplace I've never been, and what if I can't find where to get back on? But my last year's teacher, Ms. Fudman, said, "Sometimes having a good routine gives you the flexibility to try something new, and not find it scary." I still don't know exactly what she meant by that, but for now I want to stay inside the H4 for as long as the driver will let me.

When we stop at Children's Hospital, I look across the aisle and across the street at the people waiting for the westbound H4—and see a coat that looks a lot like Guillermo's.

At one of my bat mitzvah lessons, Josh said he believes God is always there for him no matter what, and he finds that comforting. I don't know if I believe in God, but I know I believe in Guillermo, because I've met him and talked to him (and he has talked to me), and whether that coat belongs to him or not, Josh is right: it is nice to remember he's around here somewhere.

Brookland Station is the last stop, and I see signs leading down to part of the station where people access the Metro trains.

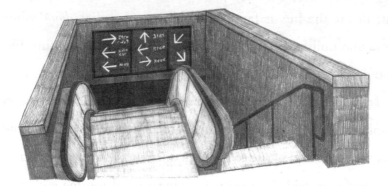

An image pops into my head of Joseph in the underground pit—only with an escalator leading down and a staircase leading back out. I take a deep breath and step carefully out of the H4.

I'm thinking about that coat of many colors that I saw from the bus. If it wasn't Guillermo wearing it himself, who was it? Did whoever was wearing it find it, bloodstained, at the top of a pit like this? What if Guillermo and Josh and my mom all disappeared in a pit? Then the H4—the only comfortable place for me on the whole earth at this moment—would just be one more prison and I'd be left like Joseph in the Torah story, alone in the world with nonsensical dreams about cows.

With nowhere to go, I stop where I am, on the stairs leading down to where people can tap their DC One cards to get to the train platform. But no matter how much I scream, the panic does not get even a little smaller.

BOOTH

Something that occurs to me mid-scream that is actually a connection to the regular world: I need to use the bathroom.

In my head, I'm saying, "Excuse me, can I please use the bathroom?" But I'm not sure if those are the same words coming out of my mouth.

One difference between being a cute little kid who needs the bathroom versus an almost-grown-up or anyway not-cute-and-tiny teenager who also needs to use the bathroom is that one leads to people wanting to help you and the other, for some reason, makes people look from side to side as if this is a very complicated problem they have never thought about before.

Maybe this Metro employee, whose name I don't know, is nervous because her rule book doesn't cover the situation of someone old enough to take the Metro by themselves but who might still need the bathroom. If this moment were calmer, I might suggest that Metro just needs a longer rule book, to cover more situations.

She is moving her mouth like she is talking, except I don't hear any sound coming out because of the noise of the Metro trains, except the Metro trains are making a noise different from their usual noise, more like screaming.

Or maybe I am the one who is screaming.

When she asks about my parents' phone number, I show her the card I keep in the little pouch with my DC One card. The Metro booth has a landline phone that is not out of battery.

I am surrounded on all sides very close and there are a lot of screens to distract me.

I don't know how long I am there. The panic still has not gone away, but it folds itself back up in a neat little package, like the cloth in my Marvin's Magic Set with twenty-seven magic tricks, many of which require you to hide something behind a cloth. When the cloth is not being used to hide something, it folds nicely into a square that I can feel inside my jacket pocket. My panic is kind of like that, when I'm not using it.

Right now my panic is not all the way folded up, but it is rumpled and tired like it needs some air before it goes back in the Marvin's Magic Set box. That's where it is when my mom walks in.

"Oh, Gilah!" she says, giving me a hug. And then "But how on earth—" as if she really doesn't know how we got here, as if the whole problem didn't start from her and Josh not being where they were supposed to be.

"Where *were* you?" I demand, not leaving the Metro booth.

"In the bathroom!" she answers, forgetting that if you need to talk about using the bathroom, you should not talk louder than a normal conversational tone.

But I don't say that. I say, "Well, Josh was gone, and you were gone."

She stares at me like she is really trying to understand. I remember what Guillermo told me about how upset his parents were after his bike accident, how it sometimes feels like they'll never understand. Maybe everyone has some version of this with their parents, even if everyone's version looks a little different.

I wonder if Guillermo was as scared when he fell off his bike as I was when I couldn't find the adults who were supposed to be keeping me safe.

Finally, my mom says, "So after you couldn't find us, you took the bus to Brookland."

I hate when she does that, takes something that makes perfect sense and just by saying it out loud makes it sound completely illogical. Because when she and Josh both disappeared on me, taking the very safe bus that I take twice a day anyway did not feel like an illogical move at the time.

"NEXT TIME TELL ME WHEN YOU'RE GOING TO THE BATHROOM!" I say, and this time people turn to look even though nobody cared when she yelled about the bathroom.

Then she surprises me: "OK," she says. "You're right."

"Thank you for saying that," I tell her.

"Could I leave a note on my seat?" she asks. "If I have to step away for a minute and I don't want to interrupt your lesson."

I think about it. "Can I design it?" I ask. "So I can recognize it as soon as I come down the stairs?"

"Definitely," my mom says.

She has to sign a bunch of papers before we can go home. By the time we finally get there, I need the bathroom worse than I've ever needed it in my whole life, pretty much.

TEXT

JOSH: Hey Gilah I'm so sorry!
My sister's baby came (3 wks early!) & I had to fly to California
By the time I found your number
(my contacts got all messed up last month) reception was bad
in the hospital

& by the time I could text you
It was too late, with the time difference
Really really sorry, hope you weren't waiting for me
I'll be back for your bat mitzvah Saturday
U R going to do so great!!!
GILAH:No prob
GILAH: Congrats!
JOSH: I'm an uncle!!!

The next text is a photo of the baby, and after that is one of him holding the baby. I hadn't remembered that Josh's sister was going to have a baby, or maybe he never told me, but I would probably cancel an appointment and fly to another city if Asher or Miri was going to have a baby and make me an aunt. And if I decide to have a baby someday, I bet Asher and—I'm suddenly very sure—also Miri would do that for me.

I text him back every baby-related emoji I can find (a bottle, a teddy bear, a baby chicken, or maybe a duck hatching out of an egg)—and throw in a few hearts even though of course the baby won't see them. By the end of the week, I'm exhausted. But maybe that's kind of a good thing. Because if I were more focused on the fact that my bat mitzvah is almost here, I might freak out so much that I just freeze. Or—I don't know—maybe start breakdancing on the bimah at synagogue or sing my Torah portion while everyone's dancing at the party. Or somehow prove to everyone that I'm not ready—not just for the bat mitzvah itself, but for being a grown-up.

The Friday night before my bat mitzvah, I'd like to be home in my pajamas eating pizza. But instead, there's what my mom calls a small Shabbat dinner for just family. Which is an example of an oxymoron, which is something that can't be true. Because even just my parents and siblings and four grandparents and my parents' three siblings plus spouses and my seven cousins adds up to a grand total of 22, including me.

So instead of being home in my pajamas, I am at the hotel where the out-of-town relatives are staying, and instead of eating pizza I am eating:

- matzo ball soup, with gluten-free matzo balls (minus the soup that my cousin Caleb spilled all over the carpet, which is fortunately the same color as matzo ball soup)
- chicken that is only a little bit dry, not dry enough to make me gag
- carrots that are too mushy, salad that is too pale,

and the gluten-free dessert, which tastes like it came out of a package that must have been labeled, "Mean practical joke to play on people who are gluten-free but actually like their dessert to taste like something a human being would want to eat."

(The regular dessert looks a lot better, but it's clear something is wrong because on my brother Asher's plate there is still half a dessert left over. When I ask him, he makes a gagging face and says, "Tastes like it was gluten-free or something.")

Which makes me wonder if maybe the hotel had a mix-up and if Asher's dessert was gluten-free, maybe my cousin Caleb's was actually regular, which could give him hives for my bat mitzvah tomorrow.

The hardest thing about being a grown-up is that not only do more things happen in a way that's not according to plan, but there are more and more meanings of *not according to plan*—more and more unexpected detours.

Across the buffet table I hear Miri tell my mom, "It's not my fault that the vegetarian entrees got delivered to the wrong event!"

And I hear my mom answer, "No, but you could have chosen a different week to decide to become a vegetarian."

Miri says, "I decided a month ago, but no one ever listens to me!"

I think about what Asher told me: Miri is someone who thinks the whole world, not just me in particular, is trying to make her life difficult. And how every bit of attention Miri draws to her missing entrée is one less relative paying over-much attention to me.

Knowing both of those things could be a way to make life with Miri easier. Maybe that is also one of the best things about being a grown-up: the times when a detour takes you to someplace you wanted to go all along.

SPREADSHEETS

After dinner, my mom has a whole schedule of who needs to shower when (night or morning) and makes sure everyone's outfits are laid out, including socks for my dad and brother, hose for her and Miri, and tights for me because I don't like the slimy feel of hose but tights feel OK, like each leg is wrapped in its own hug.

My mom has spreadsheets for what appetizers are being served when and who's sitting at which tables and what songs the DJ has to remember to play. The spreadsheet looks like one of the organizing tools we use in study skills class.

My dad asks if there's a spreadsheet for when he's allowed to use the men's room, which is actually not a ridiculous question, because what if he needs to go right when Papa Joel is about to slice the challah, or right when the DJ says my parents need to give a toast? But this question isn't to learn something but to give his opinion about what he thinks of my mom's spreadsheets.

My dad never actually says, "Here's my opinion on the spreadsheets," but my mom figures out just from his question that he doesn't think they're a good idea. Because she sounds mad when she says, "We still have one more bat mitzvah, maybe you can take a turn organizing one."

I'm listening from downstairs, near the air vent that Asher and Miri and I figured out a long time ago connected right to their bedroom, so if we ever want the real information on what my therapist said or what happened at Asher's kindergarten interview for Jewish day school, or how exactly Miri's science project clogged the plumbing at her friend's house—we can usually find out more from the vent than from asking our parents. It's like what we learned in school about primary versus secondary sources.

I'm alternating between listening and failing, over and over again, at my backflip: as much as I want to be upside down, my brain is keeping me right side up. When Asher comes downstairs at 10 p.m., he doesn't comment on the fact that I slid the armchair a few feet closer to the vent so I won't crash into the furniture while I'm head-spinning.

He waits until I stop and am panting on the chair.

"Nice," he says.

His voice sounds far away and very much right side up.

"Mom and Dad making this more stressful than it has to be?" he asks.

My counselor at school always says, "No one can *make* you feel anything, you can always choose to be in control." But that advice is actually not very useful most of the time. And if a kid asks you a question, you should never answer with something you heard from a grown-up.

I mean to shake my head, because another rule is that if you aren't going to answer someone with words, you should answer them with body language so they don't think you're ignoring them. Except that rule is sometimes impossible because sometimes people would actually just prefer to be ignored.

Except that people in your family, the people who care about you the most, sometimes they don't mind if you ignore or forget a rule, unless it turns out to be one of the rules they do care about, which you can only learn through something called trial and error. And I'm starting to get the sense that that's true for everyone, not just me.

So I don't answer Asher, and he doesn't mind because that's how we are together, so he says, "You're gonna do great."

"Thanks," I say. It's the same thing Josh said, and my parents, and Rabbi Lechtman, who not only officiates at bar and bat mitzvahs but also knows what to expect even more than most rabbis because his son had his bar mitzvah last year.

But Asher is shaking his head.

"I don't mean just tomorrow," he clarifies. "I mean—just, in general. You're gonna do great."

I grin then, I can't help it, even if the rule is that it's OK to be the first person in a conversation to smile but you should be careful about being the first person to grin.

Maybe—like being the person who takes the last slice of pizza—it doesn't matter who is first to grin if the other person is your brother.

Asher grabs his phone from on top of the cabinets. Then he turns back up the stairs. "Go to sleep before Mom and Dad start getting all sentimental," he says.

"OK," I say. But I stay up another hour, in case I might notice the exact second when I become a grown-up.

GUILLERMO

LA VELITA

Tía Carolina has brought my cousins
Mayra and Sofía with her.
They're at the table,
eating Panda Express.

Tía Carolina fusses over me,
drying my hair with a dish towel,
telling me I've grown taller already,
and fixing me a plate of
orange chicken and chow mein.

Tía Carolina is texting with my mother,
but when I ask her if Araceli is OK
She says, "Memo, no te preocupes,"

as she lights a velita,
and crosses herself.

Lighting a velita
and saying a prayer
means everything
is not OK.

HOMECOMING

We fall asleep in the living room,
Mayra and Sofía on the sofa,
Tía Carolina in the rocking chair,
and me on the floor.
I wake first when I hear the key
in the door,
and a slice of buttery yellow sun
cuts into the room.
"Mo-mo!"
Araceli hugs me
and lets the string of a blue balloon
loose from her little hand;
it floats out the open door
and into the sky
before my father can catch it,
but Araceli doesn't notice
because she's too busy
talking a million miles a minute,
tugging Sofía up the stairs,
to play.

UNINVITED GUEST

I forgot to ask permission
to go to Gilah's bat mitzvah
and my mother is not happy.
She said either Mayra goes with me,
or I don't go at all,
because she doesn't know
Gilah's family
and that makes her
"uncomfortable."

I don't understand
what my mother thinks will happen
and what Mayra could do about it—
she's only two years older than me
and an inch taller.
Also, my mother is always talking about manners
and Mayra isn't invited.
A bat mitzvah is not like
one of my tío's backyard fiestas
where anyone in the neighborhood

can just show up.
At a bat mitzvah,
I don't think that's
"proper etiquette."

TELÉFONO

PART I

Because Tía Carolina
is sitting right there
drinking coffee
and eating pan dulce
with my mother
I know better than
to get an attitude,
which is a good thing,
because right when
I'm leaving the room,
my father calls me
back and puts a
heavy hand on my shoulder.
"We get worried about you
riding around the city
and not knowing where you are."
I brace myself
for another lecture

on responsibilidad,

but then he pulls

a phone out of his pocket

and says it's time I had my own.

PART II

The phone is not fancy

like Mayra's,

because it's my father's old phone,

from before he upgraded.

It is black,

with a small screen crack,

and is too outdated

to handle most of the apps

Mayra recommends I add,

but it works well enough

to text my primos.

In a group text,

joking around with

Alex, Lucas, Bernardo,

and Nelson,

with Mayra beside me,

it feels almost

like I'm back in Langley Park,

sitting on the porch Sunday afternoon,

laughing and drinking horchata,

the sound of Araceli and Sofía

playing make-believe

and Mamá Tomasa in the kitchen

slap-slap-slapping

pupusas between her palms.

THE CAKE

PART I

Mayra is worried
about showing up
uninvited
and empty-handed
so I told her we could
make a cake
at our bakery
and it would be
from her
to Gilah.

My father bakes the cake
vanilla with white icing
and then tells Mayra
she can decorate it
however she wants.

"Should we write Feliz Cumple?"

Mayra asks,

and then I have to explain

that Gilah doesn't speak Spanish,

and that this is a bat mitzvah,

and what a bat mitzvah is,

and that they speak Hebrew at bat mitzvahs.

Mayra looks

the way I felt,

when I first read about all this

on Wikipedia.

"So, how do you write Happy Bat Mitzvah

in Hebrew?" she asks.

I pull out my phone

and do a search for

the Hebrew alphabet.

We study the screen

in silence.

"I don't think I can write that,"

Mayra says,

so we decide to write

"Mazal tov"

(which the Internet says means "Congratulations" in Hebrew,

and also "good luck," which is pretty handy,

having one phrase that means both)

but we use the Roman alphabet

which are the letters we use in

English and Spanish.

Mayra puts the cake into a white box

and ties it with pink ribbon,

even though I tell her

I think Gilah prefers blue.

PART II

Mayra will no longer be
an empty-handed guest
but she is still
an uninvited guest.

Unfortunately,
my only other choice
is to not go at all.

GILAH

EARLY

It's hard to sleep, wondering what could go wrong the morning of my bat mitzvah—whether my alarm will fail to go off, or I won't be able to find some part of my outfit, even though it has been laid out on my desk chair for two days. Or I won't be able to find my speech, even though a copy is folded in the pocket of my dress and another copy is in my mom's purse and a third copy is already on the podium on the bimah.

When the morning comes, though, I wake up an hour and a half before my alarm and everything I need is where it belongs. Which just makes me more stressed out, not knowing what the crisis will turn out to be.

Maybe we'll be out of my toothpaste or Asher will oversleep or Miri will be in a mood or I will otherwise have to make the best of a negative situation that's outside my control.

One thing that's mostly within my control is not throwing up, so when my stomach feels too nervous to eat I listen to my body and don't force things. Instead, I put some Rice Krispies in a plastic bag and put them in the pocket of my dress. It is actually very hard to find a dress that is fancy enough for a bat mitzvah but has pockets of any decent size.

My dad is walking around the house grinning and getting in everyone's way, accidentally opening the bathroom door while Asher's in the shower and taking the newspaper out to the garage for recycling even though nobody's read it yet.

Miri is screaming that my mom *did* say she could wear makeup to my bat mitzvah, and my mom is screaming back that she can wear makeup to the *party* but only if she stops screaming right this instant because she (Miri) is giving her (my mom) a headache.

It's kind of a typical morning except the atypical part is that at the end of the morning (in fact, at almost precisely noon, when the service ends and the big glass doors open up to the fancy kiddush lunch), I will be, according to some people's calculations, a grown-up.

As proof I'm the least chaotic person in my family, I'm the first one ready, a whole hour before we have to leave. But for the first time in my life, the rest of my family is ready early too.

We're even early enough that when Miri worries that her breath stinks and wants to stop at CVS for some mints, we actually would have had time except my mom doesn't carry money on Shabbat and my dad was rushing around so much that he forgot his wallet, so Miri doesn't get her mints after all.

"It's not my fault if everyone rushed me so much that I didn't get to use mouthwash," she says, and nobody answers.

Part of the extra time is for changing my shoes, because the plan is for me to walk to the building in sneakers and change to dress shoes when we get there.

Only the building is still locked when we get there, so we have to sit outside with my dress shoes in a plastic bag and Miri complaining that she could have slept twenty more minutes and been in a much better mood.

The rabbi smiles when he gets there, tells us we're the first bat mitzvah family to get there before him. I want to slow down, go back to the part where it seemed like a good idea to become a grown-up and invite everyone I knew including a boy I don't even exactly know except for riding the bus.

Because at this moment none of it feels even sort of like a good idea.

TORAH

The first hour of the service, when it's technically part of my bat mitzvah but nothing has happened yet to make me a grown-up, feels like it takes about a year or maybe more. Time is like that—it moves at different speeds depending on what you are doing. Time also moves slower when you're waiting to see what crisis is going to land.

But finally, Asher and Miri open the ark at the front of the room, and then it is time for me to read from the Torah.

In my hand I'm holding a yad, which means "hand," but it isn't really a hand, it's a metal pointer that points to the words in the Torah so people don't accidentally mess up the Torah with their fingerprints.

I like to imagine that maybe the Torah is particular about the circumstances in which it likes to be touched.

My hand holds one end of the yad, and the other end points to the letters in the Torah, which is basically a copy of a copy of a copy of a copy of what some people say God gave to Moses at Mount Sinai. I don't know where it really came from.

I'm singing the words in front of me—I guess, I'm not sure,

until the rabbi adjusts the microphone down a little and my voice gets louder, like it belongs to someone else. I'm supposed to be standing on a step stool but it isn't there and I've forgotten to check for it before I start singing.

I grip the edge of the table and take a deep, calming breath, then start again at the beginning.

The letters kick and flip—just like expert breakdancers—using their whole bodies to tell a story, like they've done for thousands of years.

The same story for thousands of years, but a little different each time a different voice tells it. And maybe each time a different person draws the letters on the parchment. All those people doing all that copying, and all those copies, each one needing to be perfect—although Josh pointed out to me that there are lots of ways of being perfect. Once he showed me where two different scrolls were in slightly different handwriting—each one copied by a different human being who is not the same as anyone else. After all, *unique* is not the opposite of *perfect*.

All those people, writing words that went from generation to generation for thousands of years—what are the odds that every single one of them looked up from the Torah and saw the world in exactly the same way?

Eventually, I run out of words, and the letters in the Torah stop breakdancing, but I am still standing there.

The rabbi says something nice and my parents give me a blessing, but I bet none of them have thought for a minute about the people who copied the Torah over and over and over. I know something they don't, and yet I can imagine being inside their mind and not knowing. Maybe this is what it means, finally, to be an adult.

Something else it means to be a grown-up: sometimes you have to give a speech.

From his seat, Asher gives me a thumbs-up. And when I glance at Miri I'm glad I do because she is looking up at me like I'm there on the bimah doing this thing that she'll be doing in another year and a half, when she is as much of a grown-up as me.

She doesn't give a thumbs-up or anything because that's what an older brother does. And Miri is still my little sister.

D'VAR TORAH

Under the podium, my hand makes a little thumbs-up for myself, which no one can see, while I give this speech at my bat mitzvah:

"Shabbat shalom.

My bat mitzvah portion is Vayeshev, which means 'and he lived.' I want to thank all the people who helped me get here today, including my tutor Josh, Rabbi Lechtman, and everyone else who helped me along the way. I especially want to thank my brother Asher and my sister Miri, because even though there are times that we all want to throw each other into a pit, most of the time we stick together better than Joseph did with his siblings. Also, I want to thank my parents for driving me around and always believing in me.

The part of the portion that relates to my life has to do with Joseph's coat. Some people call it the coat of many colors, but in Hebrew it's kitonet hapasim. One reason that this coat relates to my life is that when I was nine, I had a coat that I loved as much as Joseph loved his coat. Mine didn't have as many colors as Joseph's coat, but it had a lot more pockets. It had seven pockets on the outside and three pockets on the inside, and one of the pockets was even inside another pocket, which was where I kept my Pokémon cards.

Another way Joseph's coat relates to my life is that now I take the bus to school, and there's someone I sometimes see on the bus who has a colorful coat like Joseph's. Our bus only goes back and forth across Washington, not like Joseph traveling to Egypt with the Ishmaelites, but both kinds of coats are good for traveling and seeing different things.

Joseph traveled to Egypt and had to figure out how to do what he was meant to do even if he was far away from his family. I travel on the H4 to school and have to figure out what to do if something goes wrong, even if my family isn't there. One question I had about my Torah portion is if Joseph ever goes anywhere other than between Canaan and Egypt. Because I think a good thing about the bus is that once you know how to ride it, you can use it to go lots of places. That's what it means to me to become a bat mitzvah, that you're old enough to know how to go places in life, even if you don't know yet where you'll end up.

When I first started getting ready for my bat mitzvah, I wondered if it would be hard. But learning the Torah and Haftarah tropes wasn't as hard as I thought it would be—maybe because when I first learned how to read, I learned upside down. So it never seemed like there's only one way to look at things.

In life, kind of like with breakdancing, sometimes the things that seem like they're going to be easy turn out to be kind of hard. But sometimes what seems like it's going to be hard isn't as hard as it seems like.

One thing I've learned is that most people are kind of just figuring stuff out. Like even if Joseph can see the future, that doesn't prevent him from getting thrown into a pit. And most of the time, we can all find ways to help someone else in a hard situation.

Shabbat shalom."

After I finish talking, I look up at everyone for the first time. For just a second, I imagine I see Guillermo standing by the door of the sanctuary. I don't look long enough to see if it's really him, because I don't want to be disappointed if he didn't come. But like that day when I rode the bus past Children's Hospital, and I saw a boy that might or might not have been him in his coat, it's nice just to think he's nearby.

When I walk back to my seat, my foot crunches on something like stones in the desert. Inside my pocket, the little baggie of Rice Krispies has come open and there's a trail following me back to my seat.

My parents are both smiling, and my mom's eyes are even a little wet. Asher leans across Miri to punch me lightly on the shoulder, with a big smile, and after that, Miri whispers, "Great job."

No one seems to notice the Rice Krispies, which I think means they are not the day's crisis.

The first people to step on them without noticing are the people who come up to get honored because they're getting married soon. I wonder if any Rice Krispies are stuck in the bottom of their shoes, if they're going to wear the same shoes when they actually get married, and if some little piece of my bat mitzvah is going to be there at their wedding.

I wonder if I'll decide to get married someday—if there's somebody out there who will make life so much better that it will be worth having to share a bathroom and all the other things married people have to share. And if I do like someone enough to marry them, will I feel like even more of a grown-up than I do today at my bat mitzvah?

More people climb up and down the stairs to the bimah, and one by one each Rice Krispie gets pulverized into teeny, tiny crumbs that blend into the carpet.

Most of them will get vacuumed up, I know, by Charles or Santos, who clean the building and change the light bulbs and unclog the toilet when someone accidentally drops a kippah in there without meaning to.

But a few Rice Krispie crumbs might be too tiny for the vacuum. They'll be part of the sanctuary forever, proof that I was here. Proof of the exact spot (and maybe, like the paleontologists who can look at fossilized remains and figure out what some extinct animal ate millions of years ago, proof of the exact date) when I became a grown-up.

KIDDUSH

Asher made a plate with my favorites on it, so they didn't run out:

- two fruit skewers with cantaloupe and strawberries but absolutely no pineapple
- falafel balls and hummus
- egg salad that my mom made a special phone call for so it would not have any celery.

That takes some of the pressure off, knowing that even if I never made it out of the maze of relatives, I'll still get to eat.

I keep getting bonked by gigantic purses that belong to women older than fifty, who forget they are holding them and so bonk me in the side every time one of them tries to hug me, which is about every 0.7 seconds. I think the gigantic purses must be where they keep their scented Kleenex and their scented lotion and their scented hand sanitizer, which is not very sanitizing at all for people who are sensitive to chemicals.

The drink table supposedly has orange soda that my parents had to pay extra for, but I can't even get close enough to see if it's actually there let alone ask the server in the voice I have been practicing, "Could I please have orange soda with no ice?" because of the crowds of people between me and over there.

My mom tries to stay with me the whole time, because she says she is good at deflecting unwanted hugs—she said she got good at it when she was pregnant with Asher and people on the Metro used to try to pat her stomach, which is highly inappropriate. I can tell she is trying hard, but people keep coming over to congratulate her too, and some of them are people she hasn't seen in a long time, and I guess they don't realize that she also has a job to do, which is to keep me from getting hugged. Asher tries to stand guard too, but even he is no match for so many gigantic purses with so many kind regards.

Finally, Asher steers me over to where Miri is sitting with her plate and my plate of food and an orange soda with no ice. Which, on one hand, is a big relief, but on the other hand rules out one more possibility for what the day's crisis will turn out to be.

Miri's plate has about ten little chocolate pastries on it, and today nobody is going to stop her from eating as many desserts as she wants.

"You were awesome," she says. "And that's so great that your friend came. Can you introduce us?"

"What friend?" Asher asks.

"The boy from the bus. The one Gilah said she invited."

"He's here?" Asher says, looking around. "Where?"

"I totally saw him," Miri says. "Didn't you see him?"

Miri and Asher both knew who Guillermo was—and could recognize him in a crowd? My mouth is stuffed with falafel balls, but I nod. Now I know Guillermo was not an optical illusion.

Miri says, "Now I know why you've been so happy about taking the bus lately!"

Asher looks back and forth between Miri and me, like he's not sure whether to believe us.

"Well, hopefully he saw how terrific you were," Asher says. "You were way better than I was."

A giant grin takes over my face, and it pretty much stays there all afternoon. We're supposed to have four hours or so, in between the kiddush and the party, for resting, but between staying late at the kiddush and arriving early to the party, plus being filled with what a great job I'd done and that Guillermo was there to see it—I think I can be forgiven if not a lot of resting takes place.

GUILLERMO

THE BAT MITZVAH

PART I

When we arrive,
I worry I have the time and day wrong,
because the sounds from inside the room,
don't sound like a party.
It sounds like the opposite of a party.

Mayra and I slip into the room,
careful not to let the heavy door slam behind us.
There are rows of pews filled with quiet people,
and a table at the front with a star engraved in it,
which holds a very large scroll.

It is not very different from Catholic Mass,

except there's no font with holy water to cross ourselves,

and it doesn't smell like frankincense and myrrh,

which smells musky, and makes Araceli pinch her nose—

something my father scolds her for,

on account of it being disrespectful.

PART II

Gilah walks up to the front

in a dark blue dress

and begins to sing words in Hebrew.

Her voice goes up and down,

like a boat riding rounded ocean waves,

kind of like when Padre Rafael

chants the liturgy.

Just when I start to wonder

if I'll understand anything she says,

she starts speaking in English.

I hadn't really thought about it until now,

but now I realize,

Gilah must be bilingual too.

PART III

In her speech

Gilah talks about

Joseph and his coat of many colors,

José y el abrigo de muchos colores,

which is another thing we have in common,

because Catholics have that story too,

but the part that surprises me

is when she mentions the bus

our bus

and "someone" on the bus

who also has a coat of many colors.

I'm not wearing it today,

today I'm wearing my formal suit jacket,

which is getting a little short on my wrists

because it's the same one I wore to Mayra's quince,

but I feel my cheeks warm,

and expect everyone in the sanctuary

to turn and look at me,

but Gilah never says my name,

which is good,

because Mayra would have told

todo el mundo.

PART IV

After the service

we follow the crowd

who line up with plates

at tables of food.

"Look, pan dulce,"

Mayra juts her chin

in the direction of a table

with tiered cake stands

which hold desserts

I've never seen before.

I read the labels posted in front of each item;

they have names like

rugelach, babka, and sufganiyot.

I want to ask Gilah

which is her favorite, and

which I should try first.

Maybe

I can tell my father

about these new pan dulce

and we can make them

at our panadería.

KOSHER

PART I

Kosher?
¿Qué es kosher?
Mayra whispers.

When she asked the man
behind the dessert table
for milk to put in her café,
he said they didn't have milk
because it's
not kosher.

I pull out my phone
and look up the word
which means
"food satisfying the requirements of
Jewish law."

Wikipedia explains
under Jewish law
it's forbidden
to have a meal
with milk and meat
at the same time
but there's more rules than that.

Kosher means
no pork,
no shellfish,
and it means
the cake we made for Gilah
is not allowed here.

PART II

Mayra gasps
and covers her mouth.
"But we have time,"
I tell her.
We have time

to get another gift
because this isn't the party.
The real party doesn't start
until eight o'clock.
I show her the invitation.
The party is not here,
it's at a hotel on Woodley Road Northwest.
So we'd have to leave anyway.

Mayra pulls my hand
toward the door.
I never get to try
rugelach, babka, or sufganiyot.

PART III

What do we do
with this cake?
Mayra holds the box
wrapped in
pink ribbon
in her hands.

Hold onto it
for now
I say
as we stand at
the bus stop.
I have an idea
of who we can
give it to.

PART IV

He's sitting on the bench
where he usually sits
with his shopping cart
and his guitar.
He smiles when he sees me
and smiles wider
when we give him the cake.

THE GIFT

It takes us a few hours
but I finally find the gift for Gilah
at a souvenir shop in Union Station.
Painted red, blue, white, and grey,
it has spinning wheels, and
doors that open and close;
the miniature Metrobus
looks just like the H4.

GILAH

SHIRTS

We get to the party early enough that Andre is just starting to set up his spray-painting, and he lets me help set up the board with all the choices people can pick from, not just what color they want their name but what kind of writing and what kind of picture to go with it. Enough choices that if they said them all out loud, people's heads would start to hurt and everyone would just pick whatever he said first and then go home mad that they didn't get the sweatshirt they wanted.

Andre's board reminds me of a scheduling app I use on my phone, where you can pick one from here and one from there and one of those, and you don't have to decide for sure about any of them until you see how they all fit together.

We set up the boards and then he asks what I want, and I tell him. My name in blue, of course, graffiti letters like what used to be on this wall we ride past on the H4, except they first painted over it and then tore it down when they built new condos.

His board has a lot of soccer and ballet and basketball and musical notes and different things to choose from. But I can't find anything on his board that looks right for me.

Andre lets me look as long as I want while he sets up his equipment. When I still haven't decided, he says, "Hey, let me get your opinion on this one here," pointing to something in a sketchbook.

He asks like my opinion matters. Like he doesn't know I've never held a can of spray paint in my life except for that one month when I had been forced to be a Girl Scout and no one believed me ahead of time that it wasn't going to turn out well. Like even if he knew about that spray paint incident around the time of the display painting for World Thinking Day, like he wouldn't care.

He's showing me a drawing of dance moves but he made it too cartoony, too little-kid.

"You should make it more like this one," I tell him, using a felt-tip marker that's lying on the table drawing on a napkin the image that's in my head.

It's hard to explain, but something changes when I'm drawing the dance moves. It's like my fingers are actually doing the dancing. Which is maybe a small thing—maybe it doesn't matter if my whole body is dancing or just one part, like my fingers, but the feeling is one I want to hold onto for a long time.

The feeling is so good it almost doesn't matter what the picture itself looks like, but I smile when I realize Andre's nodding as he looks at the picture.

He says, "This is really good. My version had the eyes too buggy."

"Yeah," I nod. "It makes it not so babyish."

"Yeah," he says. "Tell you what, you have fun, and I'll make you up something special for your sweatshirt. Go dance and have fun, and I'll have it ready for you."

I thank him and head off to dance.

PARTY!

Everyone's looking at me, but for once it's not because they want to tell me to be quiet. For once everything is going exactly according to plan:

- lots of appetizers
- kids from school getting sweatshirts made
- me and both Mileses dropping ice cubes over
  the railing into the lobby, just like kids did at
  Asher's bar mitzvah
- breakdance music starting!
- breakdancing

Breakdancing is the best kind of dancing because everything connects to everything, it's all one big circle, and my elbows and my knees are all connected so it isn't my brain saying one thing to one part of my body while the rest of me's supposed to pay attention to something else. Not only am I one hundred percent totally in sync with the world, but everyone else is in sync with *me*, a whole circle around me, clapping and stomping their feet.

I'm as much in sync as the letters in the Torah, and if I weren't going so fast, someone could maybe take photos of me in all the poses and see if maybe my body is forming the different Hebrew letters, spelling out some message that's a secret surprise even for me.

Both Mileses are there from school, and Noam of course, and Leah, and Rylinn, who has never joined in any kind of circle as long as I've known her. But from my angle on the floor, all I see is knees, and the feet stomping up and down, and I don't so much hear the music as I feel it, coming up into me from the floor and from the kids all around me.

The kids at school are fine, but I've never had the kind of friends who I can be *more* myself around than when I'm by myself, breakdancing or doing art or even practicing for my bat mitzvah.

Or at least, I didn't used to have friends like that until I met Guillermo.

That's how I am, moving and twisting and my body doing just what I tell it to, when I feel something change, some new vibe mixed in with the music and the feet. Nothing anyone can see, but I know this vibe. It's the same vibe I had on the bus when a boy sat down next to me and it wasn't by accident and wasn't a mistake and I didn't imagine it and it just was.

Guillermo is a very special person like nobody else has ever been a very special person to me before, definitely not special the way people say it with the corners of their mouth turned up, like they want everyone to congratulate them on how sensitive they are.

Guillermo makes me feel hopeful—and what better place to celebrate hope than a bat mitzvah, which is all about the future, in a room that's a little bit dark but with bursts of bright light.

I open my eyes, since I guess my eyes had been closed, and my head is looking up toward the ceiling, and I'm finally ready to try the backflip.

Which is when I see Guillermo's face, moving his body to the last chords of the music, being one with the music—except not quite one with the music, like he would be if he were alone, because someone is next to him. And not just next to him like they happened to both be there because it was the only space left, like two people sitting next to each other on a bus because no window seats are available. This person is next to him on purpose, and I can tell by how their faces turn to look at each other, like they have looked at each other a lot of times before.

This person, whoever she is, is older than me, and definitely not in my class or one of my relatives or someone else who belongs here. She's taller than Guillermo and wearing a hot pink shirt and makeup. And then—suddenly—she's not just standing right next to Guillermo, she's dancing with him.

Or trying, at least. Mostly he seems to be stepping on her foot, but he keeps apologizing and she keeps laughing, which makes no sense to me at all. If Asher had made a million flash cards about ways a person could smile, I am positive he wouldn't have made one for "smiling like somebody keeps stepping on your foot."

When the music quiets down, it sounds like she says, "Junior, Junior, no, así no," which, like the laughing, makes no sense why she would call him Junior—but I must have misheard; she must have said something in Spanish I didn't understand.

Who is this person, and why is she at my bat mitzvah party?

And worse—while I'm busy trying to solve this very unexpected mystery on this otherwise carefully planned day, the song is getting quieter, ending I guess, and the DJ cuts in and announces it's time for cake.

I've missed my chance to do the backflip.

Everyone's lining up for cake, the kids from school and Guillermo and whoever this person is that he's with—and Asher and Miri, who didn't know this was going to be my big moment for the backflip and are lining up for cake with everyone else.

Part of me can't believe I missed the moment. But part of me also remembers my third birthday party, when a magician came with a pet rabbit and I was so overwhelmed that I ended up being the only kid at my own party who never got to pet that bunny. For all the growing up I've been doing—my whole life, and especially this past year—my three-year-old self is still somewhere inside me.

It is not my smoothest exit from a room, but I manage to make my way to the stairwell without anyone noticing, where I can cry as loud as I want without answering nosy questions from anyone else.

SAFE

When I'm sitting on the floor of the stairwell, the world feels dark and safe.

My kindergarten class had a place called the "cozy corner," which anyone could choose to go to anytime they wanted a break, no questions asked. No one my age would ever seek out someplace called a cozy corner, so a big part of life since then seems to be trying to find a place like the cozy corner that goes by a different name. Such as the name "H4."

The rule of the cozy corner was that if someone else came while you were in there, you could say nicely, "I'd like to be alone right now."

So that's what I say when Guillermo finds me in the stairwell.

The girl who wasn't invited peeks over Guillermo's shoulder. She's not that much taller than him, but she has a look like most people would look to see a girl like me hunched over in a stairwell, not like Guillermo's look at all.

She says something to him in Spanish, but he doesn't answer.

Instead, he asks me, "Gilah, are you OK? Do you want me to get your mom or something?"

The other girl says something else in Spanish, and I shake my head back and forth as hard as I can to say, no, please don't get my mom, the last thing I need is to explain who you are and who this girl is that you showed up with at my bat mitzvah.

And how trying to figure all this out caused me to miss doing my backflip.

Sometimes if I shake my head enough, it can stop any scream that might have tried to come out, but this time the scream is more powerful, and even though my arms are wrapped around my knees, so I'm kind of rocking back and forth a little, but not too much because there's not much room.

Everything that was good with Guillermo, from when I made the bus driver stop all the way through believing in his poetry, all of that happened because I was different from everyone else.

The only bad thing that has ever happened with Guillermo was something that could have happened to a million other people, like the girls in some of those teenage magazines, when it turns out I'm exactly like everyone else, in all of the worst possible ways.

I was finally on the verge of being more myself than I'd ever been with anyone else, finally about to do the world's greatest backflip in front of everyone I knew—when I let myself get sidetracked by a random girl who walked in with my friend.

I think I'm still filling the stairwell with screams, but part of me is laughing too: how ridiculous that my biggest problem now is not being different enough.

I bet Guillermo could write a really great poem about that.

GUILLERMO

FIESTA

PART I

When we walk into the
glowing multi-level lobby of the
Washington Marriott Wardman Park hotel
it doesn't occur to me right away
until I stare at the name on the wall
and remember the story Mr. Henry told me
about Langston Hughes.

"What's wrong?" Mayra asks
when I stop in my tracks.
"Hold on," I say, as I pull out my phone
and look up the hotel website.

This is the hotel.

This is the hotel Langston Hughes worked at.

They changed the name a little,

and I'm sure it didn't look like this in his day,

but my feet are standing,

maybe where his feet once stood.

PART II

I tell Mayra

about Busboys and Poets,

the poetry reading happening tomorrow,

about Langston Hughes,

and this hotel.

"It's a sign," she says.

"It's a sign you should go read your poem."

But I still feel like

just a kid,

and not like

a real poet.

Then I remember,

how Langston Hughes

was both a poet

and a busboy,

so there must be a way

I can be the many things I am,

including both a poet

and a kid.

PART III

At the service

Gilah's family all sat up front

facing the crowd

so I can say for certain

the older boy who is now coming toward me

from across the room

is Gilah's brother.

"I'm Asher. You must be Gilah's friend Guillermo,"

he says, shaking my hand.

I nod, and introduce Mayra,

who clears her throat
when I forget.
"How did you and Gilah meet?" Asher asks,
and so I tell him about the day
Gilah stopped the bus.

PART IV

There is food and music
and dancing.

Mayra and I try some of the moves
we remember from her quince,
sometimes waltzing steps
even though this isn't the right music,
and I keep stepping on her toes.
But also the choreographed moves
to her baile sorpresa
which means "surprise dance"
even though it isn't a total surprise
because everyone looks forward to it.
Mayra's surprise dance was a hip-hop song,

and our moves match the music well.

I'm lost in the beat until it fades away.

PART V

Through an opening in the crowd,

I see Gilah,

but instead of returning my smile,

she stares and then

rushes from the room.

PART VI

I hear her

before I see her.

"She's in the stairwell?" Mayra asks in Spanish,

giving me a look.

I put a finger to my lips,

we can talk about it later,

but for now

I just want to see if Gilah's OK.

I open the door
and peek outside.
Gilah is hugging her knees to her chest
on the floor at the bottom of the stairs.

She says she wants to be alone,
but I don't feel good about
leaving her in a dark stairwell by herself
at her special birthday party.

What if she hides there all night?
What if her family can't find her?

Mayra is asking me,
"What's the matter with her?" and
"Why is she crying?"
I am glad Mayra asks in Spanish,
so Gilah's feelings aren't hurt.

When Gilah starts screaming
Mayra makes big eyes at me,
and pulls my sleeves.

So we leave the stairwell,

and set the little bus on the table filled with gifts.

From my pocket,

I pull out the folded envelope

with my poem for her,

and I write a quick note on the outside of it.

Gilah's sister takes the envelope,

and promises to give it to her.

I look back at the stairwell

before we leave,

and say, "Happy Bat Mitzvah, Gilah,"

even though I know she can't hear me.

GILAH

NOTE

I don't exactly know how long I was out of the room, but it was not long enough for anyone in my family to come look for me, which they would have done if I was gone a long time. Also, when I come back, the other kids from my class are still dancing, like maybe I was just in the bathroom or something. And right when I get back it's time for the hora, which gives everyone something to focus on that isn't Guillermo or that girl he came here with. Our family joke is that people lift my Uncle Eric high in a chair at every bar mitzvah, and he always pretends like he's going to throw up, and everyone laughs.

I'm thinking that's just how it's going to be, when there's a break in the music and Miri whispers, "Your friend wanted me to give you this note."

"What friend?" I say, because the kids in my class all have names and Miri knows them.

Miri rolls her eyes like I'm being difficult on purpose, which sometimes annoys me but also means she treats me exactly like our other family members, which is OK.

I read the note:

> **Dear Gilah,**
>
> **You did a great job on your speech. I'm sorry we have to leave early. The little bus on the table is from my cousin Mayra. The poem inside this envelope is from me. Happy birthday.**
>
> **Guillermo**
>
> **PS – I have a phone now, in case you want to text: 202-555-1273**

Then I read the note again. That girl who showed up at my bat mitzvah—that girl was Guillermo's cousin.

All I can think of is I need to find Guillermo and—well, I don't know exactly what I need to do when I find him, but at least I'm clear on the first step.

I think about going downstairs to the lobby, but maybe they have security or something looking out for a 13-year-old girl/

sort-of-grown-up who looks like she might be crying at her bat mitzvah party. This time, instead of the stairwell, I go to the women's room. The hotel security people can't bother me there.

I read the note again and type in Guillermo's number.

GILAH: It's Gilah. Thanks for your note.

Just as I hit "send," someone comes into the bathroom, washes her hands, and stands at the sink for a long time while I wonder what to do next. There are rules about how long you have to wait to text someone if they haven't answered you, and even how many times you can text them total if they never answer at all. The rules are different if the person is in your family and/or if they are over forty and therefore sometimes don't notice their texts ("Mom ru picking me up?"/"Mom am I taking the bus?"/"How am I getting home????") but the rules are different in the other direction if the person is a boy (not in your family). Also, the rules change a lot. I don't want to use too many of my lifetime texts to Guillermo in case he doesn't answer and I think of something else I need to say.

Whoever is by the sink leaves, finally, but another set of feet walks in, uses the bathroom and flushes, then leaves without washing her hands. I wish I had seen the shoes in case that person and her unwashed hands turn up in line before me at the dessert buffet.

I've just unlocked the stall door when my phone pings. An answer!

There has been nobody in my whole life who I've been glad enough to hear from that I've wanted to use an exclamation point. He actually sends me five texts!

GUILLERMO: Hi. Sorry I was getting on the bus

GUILLERMO: Glad ur feeling better

GUILLERMO: Congrats on your bat mitzvah

GUILLERMO: Do I say mazal tov?

GUILLERMO: Or mazel tov??

That question makes me smile, since usually I'm the last person anyone thinks to ask about the right thing to say to somebody.

GILAH: Either's good. Thanks.

He doesn't answer for a long time, but I know he is still there because we didn't end the conversation.

GUILLERMO: Did u

GUILLERMO: Sorry, hit send too soon

GILAH: It's OK

GILAH: did i what

GUILLERMO: Did u like the poem

Poem? I look at the note again and find the part where he mentions a poem. A poem that is inside an envelope I have not opened.

POEM FOR GILAH

When I got on the bus that day
I didn't know how or what I'd say
But I met a friend when I needed one the most.
Her smile hello reminded me,
many of the best things in life are free;
like a spark of hope, a sidewalk guitarist's sweetest note,
or the perfect autumn leaf.

GUILLERMO: Gilah? r u still there?

GILAH: yes! i was reading your poem

GUILLERMO: do u like it

GUILLERMO: I mean, u probably got a lot
    of great presents at your bat mitzvah

GUILLERMO: i know it's not great
    like that or whatever

GILAH: it's amazing perfect

GILAH: no one has ever written me a poem before

GILAH: also thank u

GILAH: sorry i hadn't read it yet when i texted u

GILAH: i just saw the note on the outside 1st

GUILLERMO: u can read it whenever u want

GILAH: Kk, thanks

In my mind, wherever he is, Guillermo is smiling to be my friend.

I hear the music pounding from the other side of the wall, which might as well be on another planet.

GUILLERMO: Is the party still happening?

GILAH: Yeah

GUILLERMO: U should go back in there.

Ur an awesome dancer.

Suddenly I do want to go in there. Not one single thing in that room is breakable, and not one single person is busy doing something that dancing would interrupt. This place was made for breakdancing.

I pause for a second to make sure Guillermo agrees our conversation is over. I say:

GILAH: Thanks. Hope u have a good nite 2.

The rule is that if you've been talking to someone awhile and they say something like "have a good night" or "have a good day" or "have a good summer" without asking a question, you're supposed to say something like "Kk bye" that kind of gives them permission to go do something else. But maybe Guillermo doesn't know about that rule, or maybe there are times when that rule isn't the main one to follow.

GUILLERMO: Maybe tomorrow I'll send you a text.
GILAH: Kk

It is after ten o'clock, which is what time Andre was supposed to leave. Some kids are wearing their sweatshirts and some are hanging on the backs of chairs, but I never got mine—he said he was going to make up something special for me, and after all that I never got my sweatshirt.

"MOM!" I yell, bursting out of the women's room. My Uncle David is coming out of the men's room, and he smiles and says, "You were *wonderful* this morning," which there is just no answer to twelve hours later, so I don't say anything even though it's not fair whenever I have to look awkward just because someone else said a non sequitur.

"MOM!" I yell again, following Uncle David back to the party, "Mom, I never got my—"

And then I see her standing at the table with the presents, folding a sweatshirt that's gotta be mine, or else why would she leave it with all my gifts?

"Hi, Gilah," she says. "Is this what you're looking for?"

I unfold and see where it's got my name scrawled across the front, and on the back are little cartoon people who are drawing each other and at the same time working themselves into breakdancing moves, in one of those drawings that's like a paradox because how can they both be creating each other and also breakdancing at the same time? Like one of those drawings of a staircase that's going up and down at the same time, like the only explanation that makes sense is the one that also makes no sense.

Except when the things that make no sense actually make the most sense of all.

I pull on the sweatshirt and immediately feel more like myself, like I'd been missing a layer of skin but didn't know about it 'til now. My skin back in place, I head back to dance.

There's no circle around me, I'm kind of just dancing with everyone else, but I'm having such a good time that I dance and dance as long as the music is going, even while the DJ starts packing up his equipment.

At the end of the party, Rylinn from school says, "That was a really fun party. Thanks for inviting me."

"I'm glad you came," I say, which I don't even have to think about whether it's the right answer or not; I just say it because it's true. Rylinn and I don't usually hang out that much at school, but maybe that will change: maybe some of the kids I see every day might become just as good friends as Guillermo.

It might be fun to find out.

GUILLERMO

SUNDAY

PART I

When I wake up and smell
waffles, sausage, and eggs,
and hear the coffee machine gurgling,
and the tinny sound of
forks being set out on the table downstairs,
I remember,
today is Sunday.

Sundays my parents make a special breakfast,
and sometimes we go to Mass,
but usually only if it's a holiday,
since my mom isn't Catholic,

and my dad says
it's more important to be a good person
the other six days of the week,
than to pretend one day of the week

(and also all the good soccer games are on Sunday).

But this isn't a regular Sunday.

Today is the Sunday of the poetry reading.

Now,
instead of having days
to decide if I'm going or not,
I have exactly five hours.

Suddenly,
I don't feel very hungry.

PART II

Before I can decide,
Mayra kind of decides for me,
by asking
"What time is your poetry reading?"
Right in front of
my mother
my father
my sister
my tía,
and my little cousin Sofía.

(Although Araceli and Sofía
are not really paying attention
because they're busy experimenting with
how many waffles can fit into
a half-full cup of orange juice
without it overflowing…
It turns out,
the answer is two.)

PART III

While Tía Carolina
cleans up the orange juice spill
I give Mayra a look.

"Sorry," she says.
"I thought your parents knew.
You never said it was a secret."

My father looks up from his newspaper,
but keeps eating.
My mother stops pouring coffee,
and puts a hand on her hip.

PART IV

I pull the folded flyer
out of my pocket,
and hand it to my mother.

"Why didn't you tell us?" she says.
I shrug, but she waits for me
to translate the shrug into words.

Translating a shrug into words,
isn't always easy,
because sometimes it's a lot of words,
like when you translate
the English word *busk*
to Spanish,
and it turns into
"entretener en la calle por dinero."

PART V

I didn't tell you
because I didn't think
you'd really be interested
I didn't tell you
because I didn't think
you had time
I didn't tell you

because I didn't want to talk to you

about my poetry,

because I didn't know how,

until now.

PART VI

Tía Carolina offers to watch Sofía and Araceli

since they'd probably knock over bookshelves,

and run around, screaming their heads off

while someone's on stage.

My mother and father are taking me,

and will be there when I read,

which is a whole new level of

"I don't know if I can do this."

Because somehow

my parents hearing me read my poetry,

makes me feel even sicker,

than a room full of strangers

hearing me read my poetry,

maybe because if the strangers

don't like it,

they can just walk away,

and I'll never see them again,

but my parents

have to say something,

and what if it's like

when I played

"Twinkle, Twinkle,

Little Star"

on the trumpet

in fourth grade

and my parents told me

I did a great job,

even though I could see them

squeezing their eyes shut

every time I played

a wrong note?

PART VII

I watch a bus go by,
as I sit in the backseat with Mayra,
and think of Gilah.

A few seconds later,
my phone pings.

GILAH

GROWN-UP

In preschool, my class planted orange seeds in a container, and mine was the first plant to poke through the dirt. At home we moved the plant outside, first to a big container and then to the yard, and somehow ten years later it is still alive. It comes up to my waist now, but it's hard to know if it's still growing because I'm still growing too, even if it's not that apparent for either of us.

At least with a plant, everyone agrees which way is up: the opposite direction from the roots. But for some reason, people don't usually talk about plants "growing up," they usually just say they are growing.

I always figured that being a grown-up is knowing about as many of the rules as possible, so I won't get tripped up by the surprise ones. But maybe growing up is also about knowing that no one ever knows all the rules. And maybe that's OK too.

I knew that when I got older, lowercase-*r* rules from parents and teachers will start to go away, but the capital-*R* Rules will always be there. Nothing ever gets crossed off that list.

Except when something turns out not to be a capital-*R* Rule after all.

For example, in our basement, only one person doing floor exercises at a time is a capital-*R* Rule for safety. But for my bat mitzvah, Miri gave me a vinyl dance floor mat. On Sunday morning, I am stretched out on it working on my flexibility. Asher is on the couch playing online chess, and we are leaving each other alone.

Miri comes down to the big mat and, without saying a word, does four handsprings. *Thunk. Thunk. Thunk. Thunk.*

Mentally, I calculate the distance between us, like a problem in geometry class. Asher and I are both far enough away that we can't possibly get hurt.

We have two mats now. My sister is a Junior Olympic qualifier who can keep her round-offs on one mat, which I am not on.

So I keep stretching.

Which is when something amazing happens.

Miri pauses between round-offs and asks, "How, exactly, did you get to be friends with that boy on the H4?"

I think about when I first met Guillermo, and I think about us riding the bus together, talking and not talking about all the things we did and didn't talk about. But I don't know how, exactly, we got to be friends.

"I don't know," I admit. Miri should know by now that if Guillermo and I are friends—and I think we are—I'm not likely to be able to tell her in words how that happened.

Then, because it is polite to ask people questions about things they know about, as long as they are not inappropriate or personal questions, I ask, "How do kids on your bus become friends?"

"That's different," she says. (That makes the third back-and-forth statement in our conversation, and so far, neither of us has started screaming.)

"Why?" I ask. (Four!)

"Because most of the kids on my bus go to the same school," she says. "And we're, like, friends . . . but not the kind that would put on a suit and trek across the city to see each other."

I am so happy that she answered my question like we were having a regular conversation that I forget to think of something else to say. So Miri talks again.

"Did he think he didn't have to worry about you because—well—anyway, he could just, like, talk to you?"

"I don't know," I say again. She's stretching her arms all the way past her toes, looking like someone who could be bent all the way around like a rubber band. It is good for me to be more flexible, but it is also good that Miri is a little inflexible on certain things, such as missing a gymnastics meet. It isn't good to stretch yourself so far that you forget what your actual shape is.

Asher doesn't look up from his phone. "I think it has to do with when you saved his life that time," he says. "That kind of makes an impression."

"What?" says Miri.

"I didn't save his life," I say.

"But you could have," says Asher. "You didn't know how bad he was hurt. You did exactly what someone saving his life had to do."

"What are you talking about?" Miri says again.

Then without asking me what information I want shared, Asher proceeds to tell Miri more details about that first morning I met Guillermo than I even remembered. I guess Asher and Guillermo must have talked more at the party than I realized. But I have no idea why either of my siblings feels a great need to talk about this right now.

Miri stares at me, her eyes getting wider.

"That's amazing," she says. And "You're a hero," and "I can't believe none of us knew about this."

"Well, believe it," I say, under my breath. If I'm going to be a grown-up now, which is what a bat mitzvah is all about, doesn't that mean I finally get some privacy, that things can happen in my life without my family knowing every detail?

I guess the answer is "no," because before I can stop her Miri yells, "HEY, MOM! YOU KNOW THAT BOY…"

And soon my parents are pressing me for answers and details about a day I don't even fully remember and which wasn't even that special except for it being the first time that calling out loudly what I saw through a bus window was the right and important thing to do.

My mom says, "That reminds me of when you found and returned the lost earring in that IHOP. You didn't give up until it was reunited with its owner."

Miri adds, "And you didn't give up on finding a way to get me to that qualifying meet. Even I had given up on finding a way."

None of this is news to me, of course, but it's nice to be appreciated. And it's nice to have a break from talking about Guillermo—at least until my mom asks, "Have you called him? To thank him for coming to your bat mitzvah?"

"Text, Mom," corrects Miri. "Nobody calls anymore."

"Well, text, email . . ."

Miri giggles. "Email's if you're over forty." I smile too. I'm starting to appreciate Miri's talent for changing the subject away from me.

"Anyway, it's nice to let him know," says my mom. "No one ever minds being told it was nice they came."

I pretend I'm not listening, but really I'm thinking, "Oh! That's something I could say." Because I am much better at conversations that involve having something to say.

Upstairs, I send him a text:

GILAH: Thanks for coming to my bat mitzvah.

The next thing I do after sending the text is brush my teeth with my electric toothbrush, which makes a lot of noise especially after the battery has just recharged, so I almost miss the little ping that lets me know he texted back.

GUILLERMO: Thanks for inviting me!

**GUILLERMO: Just saw the H4 go by on my
way to 14 & V.**

**GUILLERMO: I'm on my way to Busboys and
Poets for the poetry reading—I decided to go.
Almost there.**

GUILLERMO: Nervous about going up on stage.
Any advice?

This is new: Guillermo, or anyone really, asking for my advice. What about getting ready for my bat mitzvah would be useful to him getting ready for a poetry reading? Especially: what does he not already know?

That's when I realize I know something that might help him, and I'm the only one who can make that something come true for him.

GILAH: Good luck!!!

That isn't really the thing that will help him: I'm saving that for a surprise but don't want to leave his text unanswered in the meantime. I smile as I put on my shoes and grab my DC One card.

GUILLERMO

BUSBOYS AND POETS

PART I

Ms. Díaz
is talking to
a Busboys and Poets employee
who has half her hair shaved,
and the other half
longish,
a nose ring,
and purple lipstick,
so I have to wait
until she's finished.

"Guillermo!

You made it!"

Ms. Díaz says

when she turns around.

She puts a hand on my shoulder,

"This is one of my young poets,"

she says,

and it feels like

she's put a name tag sticker

on my chest

that says "POET"

instead of "GUILLERMO."

Sometimes

the labels other people put on us

are ones we want to take off,

but this one feels like

a badge of honor,

this one

gives me a little more courage

to get up on stage.

PART II

I watch the students ahead of me

take the stage.

They are all older than me.

Some leave the microphone in the stand,

Some hold it with one hand,

Some grasp it,

like a warm cup of tea,

speak their words,

while the audience

calls out encouragement,

and snaps their fingers.

All of them seem confident,

and punctuate

their sentences

with their hands

as if placing invisible periods,

question marks,

and exclamation points

in the air.

PART III

I've only been to El Salvador once,
and I was so little,
I don't remember much about that trip,
but I remember we visited a volcano.

I was really into dinosaurs,
so I thought it would look like
the volcanoes in my picture books,
with red-hot molten lava
exploding into the sky.

We walked right up to
the rim of the volcano
and looked down into it.
The crater was just a big hole
that looked like a green valley
with dirt at its center.

"Where's the lava?" I asked.
"This volcano is dormant," my father said.

"What does dormant mean?" I asked.

"This volcano is sleeping," he said.

"But it could wake up at any time."

PART IV

A poem occurs to me,

and I ask my mom

for paper and pen,

since I don't have anything with me,

and she always has everything with her.

I write the poem quickly,

before it can leave,

because that happens sometimes,

if you wait too long.

When it's finished,

I know it's the poem I should read,

to pay tribute to Langston Hughes,

who feels like he's here in this room with me.

I go back up to Ms. Díaz,

who is standing near the stage,

and ask her if I can read a different poem

than the one I wrote for the contest.

She reads the poem

I've just written down,

and her smile gets bigger

and bigger

with each line

before she nods

and hands it back to me.

PART V

As I sit back down

with my parents to wait,

I look over by the door,

because it feels like

someone is staring at me.

That someone
turns out to be Gilah.

PART VI

My phone pings again.
The short text from Gilah says:
I believe in you.

PART VII

The poem I read. Dedicated to and inspired by
Langston Hughes:

What happens to a poem unread?

Does it disintegrate
like sugar cubes left out in the rain?
Or slice like a paper cut—
And then cause you great pain?
Does it smell like a carton of milk that's expired?

Or crackle and smoke—
like a wind-driven wildfire?

Maybe it just spills over
like an overfilled cup.

Or does it erupt?

PART VIII

"Memo, that was beautiful,"
my mother says.

My father ruffles my hair.
"If I had known you liked poetry,
I'd have shown you some Salvadoran poets,
like Salarrué, Claudia Lars, and Alfredo Espino
a long time ago," he says.

"There's Salvadoran poets?" I ask,
because the thought never occurred to me.

"Of course there are," my father says.

"In fact, the abuelo you're named after,

Papá Guillermo, was a poet.

Not famous beyond his

small town back in El Salvador,

but a poet nonetheless."

My father promises to call up some family

to see if anyone can send him copies

of my grandfather's poetry.

When I notice Gilah standing there,

I can tell by the way she's smiling

that she liked my poem.

GILAH

NICKNAME

When I get tired of standing, I retreat to the bookstore area and slink down on the floor so my back is leaning against one of the shelves. From this angle, the words surround me just like music surrounds me when I'm breakdancing, just like the glider swing surrounds me in the basement. Just like I'm surrounded when I'm on the bus.

After Guillermo's poem, I'm surrounded by the sound of applause, and my hands are joining right in. I stand up so he can see me, even though I'm not so surrounded anymore, and that's when one word zings across the not-very-big distance between the performers and the audience: Memo.

I'm sure his mother (I think that must be his mother) called him "Memo," like a paper in an office—which is not only not his name but not even a name at all. Surely his mother must know that. Also, if she was the one who picked out his original name, something as nice as Guillermo, why would she call him something else?

Guillermo smiles, and it's a smile from near the very end of Asher's flash card deck, where the smiles get more complicated. This smile shows that his feelings aren't hurt, they're in on the same joke.

I slink back down on the floor, surrounded by bookshelves, surrounded by words: thousands, maybe millions, of different words in all of these books, and even more words in my ears as the event ends and people all over the store and the restaurant put even more words in the air. Maybe we need so many words because sometimes really important things are complicated enough that one word isn't enough.

Maybe I am complicated enough to need more than one word.

I remember the day Guillermo tried to give me a nickname: Laa-laa, which I think was one of the Teletubbies and also sounds like loud singing, or Gilita, which is just adding an extra letter to a whole other name, Galit, so I think does not technically qualify as a nickname. I didn't think I wanted a nickname then: I am one person with one name and people are complicated enough without changing around what we call them.

But Guillermo's mother calls him Memo (however that's

spelled)—and then I remember hearing Mayra call him "Junior," which I didn't mishear after all. It was yet another nickname.

Maybe I am actually one person with many parts. And maybe it is actually less complicated when people call the different parts of themselves by different names.

But if I'm not Laa-laa or Gilita, which is the part of Gilah who made a new friend, all by myself while traveling across the city on a Metrobus? And what could my nickname be?

In front of me is a shelf full of travel books, other places I might like to visit, by bus or train or plane or boat. There are a lot of books about Mexico, which I remember is where Gila (pronounced *Hee-la*) monsters live.

I am definitely not a monster, but Gila monsters do have the admirable quality of blending into their surroundings by being a lot of different colors at the same time. They're different from chameleons, who change colors to blend in, but can actually be a lot of different things at the same time.

Kind of like people. Kind of like me.

I wave to Guillermo, who gives a little wave back, but he is surrounded by a lot of people, and I remember how that felt yesterday—though it's hard to believe my bat mitzvah was just yesterday.

On the bus ride home, I send him a text. I start to type, "I have an idea for a nickname." But then I remember that it is polite to start with what the other person is likely to be thinking about, when I can figure that out, which right now I can. So I edit my text before hitting send.

> GILAH: U did a great job. Also I have an idea
> for a nickname.
>
> GUILLERMO: Cool. What is it?
>
> GILAH: Does Gila, like the lizard, count
> as a nickname if it's pronounced "Heela?"
>
> GUILLERMO: Sure ... Want me to start calling
> you that?

I think about Guillermo calling me by my new nickname the next time we see each other on the bus: Gila with the *G* pronounced like an *H* because the word is actually Spanish. Gila like Heela, with the *H* from the end of my name, where it had always been silent, moved up to the front of my name, where it has its own sound.

That day I first saw Guillermo, maybe it was actually Gila, rather than Gilah, who knew that it's good not to be silent.

NO POINT

In some ways there is no point to having a bat mitzvah, because even if it's about becoming a grown-up I am actually still a kid.

But then I find something in our living room that makes me think maybe there's a point after all.

It's a printed-out brochure about a breakdancing camp happening this summer. Here is some of what they have at this camp:

- Breakdancing techniques
- Breakdancing drills
- Advanced breakdancing moves

And here is what they don't have at this camp:

- Study skills
- Social learning
- Any skills that are really a code for "we're using this as therapy to teach kids on the spectrum to be more like other people"

Nobody in my family claims to have any idea how the brochure got in our living room, which is strange because what are the chances that my mom had a friend over during the day who just happened to lose these papers out of her bag? Also, I notice that the papers don't look crumpled like the ones I lose out of my bag.

The kids in the pictures look like they're having fun. In one picture the kids are outside eating lunch, and in another picture they're gathered around some of their classmates doing some kind of demonstration. I'm already thinking about how, if I go to this camp, I could make a little checklist or something of what do to at lunch and what to do if there's a big-group demonstration. I could handle that, I think. Because in all the other pictures they're dancing, glad to be together but focused on what they're working on. Like Guillermo did that time he was so focused on writing a poem that he almost missed his stop.

The pictures show just kids, but I'm pretty sure the adults are just outside the camera frame, there to help people breakdance safely—not making sure that everyone's talking the way they're supposed to be or giving out tokens for making eye contact.

The kids in the picture look so focused, they probably wouldn't pressure me if I didn't feel like talking right then or if whatever I said wasn't an exact copy of everyone else.

Maybe one of those kids in the brochure would even turn out to be a friend like Guillermo.

BIRTHDAY

A week goes by, and the excitement of my actual thirteenth birthday is pretty much nonexistent as compared to my bat mitzvah. I can't even listen to hip-hop music, because it makes me think about the backflip I didn't do.

I borrow the step stool from the hall closet and carefully climb up so I can take down the printouts from my closet. I feel a little dizzy up there, so I don't stay long, just take the printouts down and wait 'til I'm back on the ground to peel off Miri's blue putty and leave it in a nice, neat ball on my dresser. (That's something I might not have thought of doing before my bat mitzvah, I might have put the putty into the recycling with the printouts, so maybe I am a grown-up now after all.)

Miri is not home when I do this. She is in Baltimore, at her gymnastics qualifying meet, which she got to attend thanks to my creative thinking and recognition that, like most things in life, there is not just one way to accomplish something you want to do. That night, I'm in the basement listening to my flip music but not actually flipping when I hear Miri come in with my dad.

"I qualified!" she yells happily. Which, if you know Miri, you know her yelling happily is highly unusual. Unusual enough that I venture up the stairs in time to see her hug my mom. And my mom looks happy too. That's another smile I could add to Asher's diagram: smiling because you're really happy for someone.

Asher also isn't home—he is out with Michaela—and my dad already knew her good news because he was in Baltimore with Miri. So if Miri had to yell when she came in, she probably wanted someone other than my mom to hear.

Miri was yelling her good news for my benefit.

"That's great, congratulations!" I say.

Miri looks back and forth from my mom to me, and my mom looks back and forth from Miri to me, and while we're all standing there, Miri announces, "Dad and I stopped for dinner on the way home."

Then she pauses. "It wasn't at an IHOP."

For a second, I'm really surprised: I'd always thought we both love IHOP equally and that that was one of the few things we have in common—but maybe Miri just needs to speak up in a positive way about her feelings because the rest of the world is not full of mind-readers. Maybe that is something I can teach her when she's ready.

I realize I am OK even if we don't love IHOP equally.

But then I'm really-really surprised. Because Miri says, "Dad suggested it, but I said I wanted to wait 'til you could be there too."

"For real?"

"It wouldn't have been the same without you!" Miri says.

After Miri goes upstairs, I go back downstairs to turn my music up louder. I guess if I were great at being a grown-up, I would look around to see what my mom was doing in the kitchen and ask if I could help her somehow. But I don't feel like helping in the kitchen; I feel like listening to my music. And I've only been a grown-up for, like, a week, so I think there is probably some sort of grace period.

THE NEXT SECTION

After a while I turn off my music and just listen in my head. The lights are off too, like I like them sometimes, and I am stretched out on the floor, my back against the sofa, listening to music in my head in a way that might not be clear to people who didn't see me.

Miri turns on the light and does, like, twenty one-handed cartwheels.

When she sits down on the couch across from me, she says, "Hey."

"Hey," I say. "Congratulations on qualifying. I know you worked super-hard." And I don't add, "I'm glad I thought of you going to that other meet." Because a nice part of being a grown-up, it turns out, is all the things that really aren't about me at all.

"Thanks," she says.

I'm pretty sure the answer is not "You're welcome," but this is one of those times when knowing what the answer isn't just leaves me with a big gap and no answer at all.

But then Miri says, "Why did you throw away those breakdancing printouts I gave you?"

"First of all, I didn't throw them away; I recycled them."

I pause.

"But *you* gave those to me?"

She shrugs.

"I knew you'd think it was Asher. But why did you recycle them?"

I'm still thinking about this news, but I am also trying to keep up my end of the conversation.

"I saved your putty," I say, testing to see if this is one of those times when you can answer a different question than what someone asked.

Miri sighs. "WHY did you recycle the backflip printouts?" (Oh. It was not one of those times.)

"I didn't need them anymore," I say. "I didn't do the backflip at my bat mitzvah."

"Can you?" she says.

"My bat mitzvah's already passed," I remind her.

Big SIGH again. "Can you DO the backflip? Let me see you."

I'm not ready for this. I'm really not ready for this, but look how ready I was at my bat mitzvah, and that didn't do me any good. I wasn't ready to meet Guillermo, and that turned out OK. Maybe there are different ways to think about being "ready."

Maybe later I'll take the printouts from the recycling bin and put them back up with my special gold thumbtacks. I know all the pictures already in my head, but maybe I wouldn't mind seeing them outside my head sometimes too.

For now, I look at Miri, who's smiling and giving me a thumbs-up from down on the floor, where she's ready to spot me.

So I pump my music up loud and without looking at her or anything else, I take a few minutes to stretch and then pretty much become the kid in the diagrams, the one I've been trying to be all this time. I take a running start, and with the strength of the whole Hebrew alphabet underneath me, boosting me up and rotating me through the air—I do my backflip.

I'm flying through the air just like Guillermo flew through the air that day of the bike accident, only his meant that things were out of control and mine means that things are finally, at least for this moment, totally within my control.

When I look up, not only is Miri clapping for me, but the rest of my family has gathered on the steps—maybe they knew from the music that something was about to be happening down here.

My mom is clapping, and Asher is wooting, and my dad is grinning like I've made him proud.

Here is the best part about flipping, the part I didn't even know to expect: when I get a view of my family—the people I'm used to thinking of as my regular, right side up, fitting-right-in-with-everyone family—this time they're the ones upside down.

And they're cheering for me.

I am upside down and backward, but my family understands I've got things right.

Maybe they understood all along.

All this time, I knew that some things some people find easy are things I find hard. But how great is it that some things other people find hard—such as screaming on a bus if necessary for the safety of someone who might become my friend!—well, those things might not be exactly easy for me, but they are something I know I can do when there is an important reason.

After all, the earth has rotated on its axis eight times since my bat mitzvah, 365 times since my last birthday, and 4,748 times (including leap years) since I was born. And at every single moment, there's been someone on the exact opposite side of the earth. I always used to think that if someone on one side of the earth was right side up, then someone in another hemisphere had to be upside down. But really we are all right side up. And the sooner everyone realizes that, the better for everyone.

GUILLERMO

BOXES

PART I

My mother has been cleaning the house

in preparation for all the family and friends who will

come to eat

and exchange gifts on Nochebuena this year,

including Mr. Henry,

and Gilah's family,

(except I will wrap a gift for her in Hanukkah paper,

and offer them vegetarian tamales without lard in the masa,

which wouldn't be kosher).

And when my mother cleans,

somehow we all end up cleaning, too.

Araceli is supposed to be wiping the windows,

but instead she is huffing breath onto them,
and drawing pictures with her finger
in the fog.

I am supposed to be emptying the cardboard boxes
in the upstairs hallway,
which have been sitting here since we moved,
and have MEMO written on them
in black marker.

In the boxes I find
stuffed animals I won at a carnival,
a blanket my abuela made me,
two pairs of shoes that don't fit me anymore,
a yellow participation ribbon for my seventh-grade
science fair project,
a few board games,
a dozen books,
Araceli's plastic tiara (which I throw toward her bedroom),
Araceli's cat-shaped keyboard that meows (which I keep),
a broken pair of sunglasses,
Legos,

a calculator,

a compass,

a harmonica,

a solar-powered dancing flower,

a telescope,

a DC United scarf,

and

my winter coat.

PART II

My winter coat is black and grey

like the dirty snow

on the sides of the street;

unmemorable,

unremarkable,

unexceptional,

unlike

my father's coat of many colors.

Memories of Maryland,

and adventures with my cousins

are connected
like the links in my bicycle's chain
the same way
memories of DC,
and learning to make it my new home,
are woven like a thread
into the fabric of
my father's coat of many colors.

Maybe I'll wear it,
a little while longer.

Maybe I'll put my winter coat
back in the box.

ABUELO

I never met my abuelo Papá Guillermo,
I just knew that he was Mamá Tomasa's husband,
and he had died before I was born.

Now I have his poems spread out before me,
and am learning so much about him
through the words he left behind.

Maybe someday
future generations of my family
will learn about me
through the poems I have written,
and they'll say,
he was a poet
not famous beyond
Washington, DC,
but a poet nonetheless.

DECEMBER

December is
visits from family,
tamales wrapped in wet, green banana leaves,
turkey sandwiches on French bread from our bakery,
the scent of pine in the living room,
and the glint of silver tinsel.

December is
feathery snowflakes on window panes,
clear night skies and bright stars,
red velvet bows on lampposts
and white lights wrapped around bare branches.

December is
the bus sloshing through slush puddles
on my way to ice skate
in my coat of many colors
at the National Gallery Sculpture Garden
where Gilah is waiting for me.

ACKNOWLEDGMENTS

Pamela Ehrenberg wishes to thank so many, many people who supported us during this book's seven-year journey to publication. I am thankful most especially to:

Tracy, of course, for elevating the whole experience beyond what a single brain or heart could have accomplished. What a gift to have someone who cared about my messy rough drafts as deeply as I did—and who happened to have the organizational gift to help me keep track of them! Thank you, above everyone, for making this book a reality.

Gabe Lechtman, for his feedback on an early draft and his belief that this story is important, and also to his mom, Jolie, for coordinating the emails and for the window into their family's joy.

Two writing groups, including Elizabeth, Emily, Farrar, Gwen, Kirsten, and Meredith, as well as Caroline, Erica, Kate, Kristin, and Tammar.

Lyn Miller-Lachmann and Rabbi Ruti Regan for their insightful guidance. Hopefully, their wisdom brought us closer to our goal of storytelling that is accessible and empowering for all readers—including and especially those who will carry the torch forward to tell their own ever-better stories in the future.

Quique Aviles, whose blessing launched the journey.

The Adas Israel community—partners and models in the journey toward inclusivity. And especially Rabbi Kerrith Solomon, who was not surprised at all by my own journey during the writing of this book.

Dr. David Black at the Center for Assessment and Treatment, who helped generate some answers but many, many, many more questions.

Rachel Papantonakis, whose pandemic-era research mission ensured the accuracy of the Brookland Metro station.

Transit workers in DC and elsewhere who keep our communities functioning in a pandemic and in what passes as day-to-day "regular life" for so many of us.

Those who cared for and nurtured me these past seven years so that I could care for and nurture the book—my parents, David and the late Joan Grebow; my in-laws, Randy and Ronald Ehrenberg; the family members who are friends; the friends who are family; and the colleagues at (and through) the National Association for the Education of Young Children who have taken on elements of both.

Nathan, who sat beside me on the H4, and Talia, who rode the D2—the two people on earth I will detour with anywhere, any time at all, always.

And, Zev, for stopping the bus, and his family, for agreeing to let others be inspired by your heroism. I can't wait to hear what you do and whom you inspire next.

• • •

Tracy López wishes to thank, first and foremost, my co-author, Pamela Ehrenberg. I'm so thankful our paths crossed, and that I had not only the opportunity to create this world with you, but become your friend. I don't think I'll ever look at an onion again without remembering how you, more than anyone I know, are particularly adept at peeling back layers I didn't even know were there.

To my husband Carlos, immeasurable gratitude for making it possible for me to write at all by keeping a roof over our heads. Thank you for being the practical one and letting me do what I love. Te quiero mucho. To my boys, Nicolas and Julian: you grew up too quick for me to read this to you as a bedtime story, but I hope you like it anyway. To Mercedes, mi suegra, gracias por enseñarme tanto de la bella cultura salvadoreña para que pudiera escribir historias como esta y familias como la nuestra puedan verse en las páginas de un libro.

Eternally grateful to my parents Rick and Susan Ennis—for raising me in a house full of books, trips to the library, and encouraging my creativity—and to my sisters Katie Ennis and Jamie Antoun for the childhood memories I get to draw from every time I sit down to write. To my Grandma Trudy, Grandma Shirley, and other family members who never stopped asking how the book was coming along—thank you for motivating me to keep at it.

Thanks to Chico (rest in peace) and Margot, writing buddies who never failed to keep me company and always seemed to know when I needed a break to play fetch.

To my agent Marietta B. Zacker, a debt of gratitude for all your help, and guidance. Many thanks as well to Angel Magaña, Nydia Rivera, and Marcus K. Dowling for your valuable feedback. To Alberto Ferreras and Rachel Keener who both generously took the time to give me writing advice many years ago; I've never forgotten, and will always pay it forward.

Abrazos y agradecimientos to Carrie F. Weir, Ana Flores, Melanie Edwards, Claudia Mayorga-Del Cid, Jaime Flores, and so many other friends who offered encouragement over the years.

My humble respects to Langston Hughes for endless inspiration, Duke Ellington (with apologies for Mr. Henry's rendition of "Take the A Train"), and Chuck Brown & The Soul Searchers, whose go-go music was a frequent soundtrack while writing.

And to my critique partner and best friend, Aisha Saeed: I literally would not be here without you. You have been there for me through many years and many manuscripts that I would not have finished (or started for that matter!) if I hadn't known you were waiting to read them. There's no one else in this world who knows my writing mind like you. You are a blessing I count daily.

• • •

Both authors would like to give a huge thank you of course to the PJ Publishing team: our editor Karen Ang, whose impressive organizational skills, expertise, and positive attitude made the revision process a pleasure; Catriella Freedman who believed in our project from the very start; as well as Rachel Goodman, Madelyn Travis, Michelle Moon, and others behind the scenes for their hard work getting us to the finish line. To art director Chad W. Beckerman, and our talented illustrator Laila Ekboir we owe a debt of gratitude for our stunning more-perfect-than-we-could-have-imagined cover and illustrations.

Our appreciation as well to the D.C. Commission on the Arts and Humanities for their generous support of this project.

Lastly, our thanks to you. Writers are not much without readers, and we're honored that out of the millions of books to read, you read this one.